CW01500424

HAPPILY EVER AFTER IN HOPE COVE

Rebecca Paulinyi

"Googled" a book on Hope Cove for You. It's so dire Amazon didn't want it returned :) charity shop?

Copyright © 2024 Rebecca Paulinyi

All rights reserved

This is a work of fiction. Names, characters, businesses, places, events and incidents are either the products of the author's imagination or used in a fictitious manner. Any resemblance to actual persons, living or dead, or actual events is purely coincidental.

No part of this book may be reproduced, or stored in a retrieval system, or transmitted in any form or by any means, electronic, mechanical, photocopying, recording, or otherwise, without express written permission of the publisher.

Cover design by: GetCovers

*For Joyce, who loves reading about Devon
and knits the best baby clothes!*

CONTENTS

CHAPTER ONE

When Hannah had last glanced at the clock, it had been two hours after her shift had ended – and yet the patients just kept coming. Another doctor had called in sick, and she couldn't possibly leave with the backlog of patients she had to see.

"Dr Martin, could you just have a look at the man in bed three when you have a second?" a nurse called over. "He says the pain is worse, but we've already given him painkillers."

"I'll add him to my list," Hannah replied. It was a good job there was no one waiting for her at home. It was going to be a long afternoon.

When she'd finally changed out of her scrubs and shoved her mousy brown hair back into a ponytail, she glanced at the clock again. Just gone seven – no wonder she was hungry. She hadn't eaten since lunchtime, when she'd shoved down a stale cheese sandwich, and she'd not sat down since.

Being an A&E doctor certainly wasn't for the faint-hearted – but there was nothing else she would rather be.

She'd dreamed of being a doctor since she was a little girl. One of the boys in her year one class, whose face she could still clearly picture, had told her that only boys could be doctors.

Her parents had told her it wasn't true, but that

comment had only added to her determination.

"We're heading out for some food and drinks," Jasmine, a doctor from the oncology ward who Hannah had known for years, said as she entered the break room. "You coming?"

Hannah thought for a moment. She was exhausted, but starving too. There was probably no food in at home, and sitting and eating a take away alone didn't hold much appeal.

"Go on then. As long as we eat first – I'm starving, if I drink now it'll go straight to my head.

Jasmine laughed. "Food first. Promise. Meet me outside in ten? I just need a quick shower."

Hannah hurried out through the bustling A&E with her head down. There was always so much to be done. She loved her job, but she couldn't give it any more hours than she already did. And if she saw someone who needed help, she knew she would struggle not to be sucked back in...and then she'd never eat.

The January evening air was bitter, and she pulled her coat around her as she exited through the automatic doors. It was so stuffy in the hospital that she welcomed the fresh air, even if it made her shiver. She tried to remember if she'd set the timer on the central heating in her flat. She was out at such unpredictable and changing times that there wasn't usually much point – but it was nice to come home to a warm flat when she did remember.

The automatic doors slid open to let out a group of chatting, laughing doctors and nurses, and Hannah moved to join them.

"Long night?" Tim, a nurse from the pediatric ward, asked her.

"Aren't they all?" she said with a laugh. "And I'm fed up of coming out to pitch dark. Spring can't come soon enough!"

The five of them walked down the dark street, sharing stories of the highs and lows of their days.

Hannah loved helping people, she loved solving a medical mystery, and she loved the camaraderie of the hospital staff. She'd worked in the same hospital since her foundation year five years earlier, and most of the group of friends she had had started then, or been there even longer than she had. Only Eloise, an F2 doctor with a wicked sense of humour, was new to the group. There were enough of them that there was always someone to go and get a drink or something to eat with, no matter what time her shift ended.

"Did you hear the gossip about Mendez?" Tim asked as they took a seat in their usual booth at the local pub.

Hannah frowned and shook her head. "I don't think so..."

"Apparently he and Lisa Simmons, the blonde nurse on cardiac, are an item," Jasmine joined in.

Hannah's frown deepened. "I thought she was married?"

"So did we," Eloise said. "But now no one knows if they're having an affair, or if her marriage had already crumbled."

"It's certainly not easy to keep a relationship going with the hours we work," Duncan, a fellow A&E doctor, said.

"Yeah, my Jack is always complaining at how little time we have together," Jasmine said with a sigh.

"One-night-stands all the way," Eloise said, sipping the pint she'd ordered before even looking at the food menu. "That way, no one is disappointed, no one is complaining when work is all you can think about..."

Tim laughed. "You're young, El. The one-night-stands get tedious after a while, believe me."

"Is Michael okay with the night shifts and all the hours you work?" Hannah asked, curious.

Tim shrugged. "It's not ideal, but he knew what I did when we met. Love finds a way..."

They all ahhed, while Eloise made sick noises. The conversation was interrupted when the waitress came over, and Hannah ordered a lasagna with extra chips. She was starting to feel a little lightheaded.

"What about you, Han?" Duncan asked. Hannah knew he had separated from the mother of his child the previous year, and so doubted Tim's starry-eyed view of romance fitted with his current worldview.

"You sound like my parents," she said with a laugh. "I guess...it would be nice to have someone to go home to. But I love my job too much. I'm not willing to cut back on my hours or compromise...so I guess an empty flat and dinners for one are staying for the foreseeable future!"

She laughed. Her parents were always asking her when she was going to settle down, especially since she had turned thirty. They didn't seem to understand that, right now at least, her job was the most important thing in her life. She had worked extremely hard to get where she was, and she wasn't going to let anything or anyone get in the way of her becoming an A&E consultant.

After dinner, Tim and Jasmine disappeared to return home to their significant others, and Duncan decided he fancied an early night. Even though she was exhausted, she joined Eloise at the bar for a drink, and they were soon joined by two guys who were keen to buy them another round.

"What are two lovely ladies like you doing alone on a Friday night?" the younger of the two, a classically good-looking blond guy with gleaming white teeth, said as he joined them at the bar.

"Just finished a long shift," Eloise said. "And haven't found anyone worth spending time with yet."

"Well hopefully we can change your minds..."

Thankfully, the dark-haired man who sat down next to Hannah didn't seem to be so keen on cheesy chat-up lines.

"Where do you work?" he asked, flagging down the barmaid and ordering them both another drink.

"Just at the hospital down the road," Hannah said. "I'm an A&E doctor."

His eyes widened, and Hannah wasn't sure if he was impressed or intimidated. It certainly wasn't only men who could become doctors, but it did seem to make some men feel slightly on the back foot.

"And what do you do?" she asked, sipping her vodka and coke.

"Nothing so selfless, I'm afraid," he said with a self-deprecating laugh. "I'm in finance." He held out his hand to shake hers. "Jimmy," he said.

"I'm Hannah," she said, taking his hand. He was good-looking and had a deep, attractive voice. She certainly wasn't against having a drink or two. "And this is Eloise, a colleague of mine at the hospital."

"That's Tom," Jimmy said, nodding his head towards the blond. "But I think we may have lost them..."

Hannah laughed as Eloise dragged Tom onto the makeshift dance floor. It wasn't even nine, but she'd had a few drinks since her shift had ended and was clearly in the mood to have some fun.

"It looks like it."

"So," Jimmy said, taking a swig of his beer, "what do you do when you're not saving lives?"

"Sleep," Hannah said with a laugh. She knew he was expecting some sort of hobby or interest, but the truth was, she didn't really have any. She loved her job and put in far more hours than she was paid for. At the moment, that was enough.

"Well, if you get a break in your busy schedule, maybe I could take you out sometime," he said with a grin. "Somewhere with tablecloths that does better food than this place."

Hannah laughed. "That would be nice – but I don't know my schedule very far in advance. And I have to say, I don't mind the food this place serves."

"Well, you'll be an easy date to impress then if you think this place is good."

She stayed for an hour, flirting with the cute guy and drinking one too many vodkas. It turned out he was a bit of a foodie and had a lot of opinions on restaurants in the city. She realised how little she went out anywhere that wasn't close to the hospital and convenient, so she couldn't contribute much to that conversation.

Just before eleven, the bell rang for last orders. "I'd better be getting home," Hannah said, grabbing her phone to order a taxi.

"I know a place that stays open later if you want to continue the evening..."

Hannah shook her head with a smile. He was sweet, but there was no spark between them – and it had been a very long day. "Thanks, but I'm exhausted."

"Fair enough. Here, have my number." He pulled

a business card out of his pocket and handed it to her. "When your schedule has a space, let's see if we can do that dinner. I promise I'll take you somewhere nice."

Unsure if she would ever see him again, Hannah pocketed the card. "Thank you – and thanks for a lovely evening."

He leaned in for a goodnight kiss, which he clumsily pressed somewhere between her cheek and her lips.

She felt nothing, which only confirmed that although he was pleasant enough to chat with, there was no point in pursuing anything further. Even if she had time, which she definitely did not.

Eloise, on the other hand, looked very cosy with Jimmy's blond friend, and when Hannah motioned that she was about to leave, Eloise just waved goodbye.

Thankfully, it wasn't raining, because that always made getting a taxi impossible. She normally took the Tube to work, but she was tired and wanted a quick journey home.

When she got back to her dark flat, which was chilly – she had definitely forgotten to set the timer on the heating – she decided to skip a shower and jump straight into bed. Her body and mind were weary, and thankfully she had a day off the following day, so there was no need to set an alarm or worry about being ready for work at some godforsaken hour. No, she could let the vodka lull her to sleep and sleep off its effects the following morning.

Hannah was still asleep when her phone rang the following morning. At first, she tuned it out, thinking it was her alarm. When she forced her eyes open, her head feeling a little sore, she realised it was ringing and answered it before thinking better of it.

"Hello?" she said, her voice a little scratchy.

"Hannah, dear? Were you still asleep? It's nearly ten o'clock. I didn't think you'd possibly still be in bed."

Hannah fumbled on her bedside table for the bottle of water she kept there and tried to get rid of the desert-like feeling in her mouth before replying. "Late night, Mum."

"Well, I'm sorry to wake you. You know, you really should put your phone on silent if you're going to sleep past ordinary hours."

Hannah would have thought, considering how often she did night shifts, that her mother might have just learnt to message instead of ringing – but there was no point in saying that now.

"Everything all right, Mum?" she asked, propping herself up a little on her pillows. She didn't feel terrible, but the extra-long shift had made her body ache, and her head throbbed with one too many vodkas in her system. Thank goodness she had nothing on that day – well, except for a talk with her mother, apparently.

"Oh, nothing, just ringing for a chat. Haven't heard from you in a while."

There was a hint of guilt-tripping under the calm, breezy words that made Hannah sigh. "Sorry, Mum. Work's been crazy, you know."

"Work's always crazy, darling. It has been since you were in university. Surely there has to come a point where it calms down?"

Privately, Hannah did not think the life of a doctor ever really calmed down – well, at least not to the level her retired mother would think was acceptable. But perhaps once she was a consultant, her hours wouldn't be quite so insane.

"Were you out late working?" Mum asked.

"Uh – no. I pulled a double shift until seven, then joined some friends after work for drinks."

"Well, I'm glad to hear you're socialising. Although friends aren't the same as having a husband, you know. You're thirty now, your biological clock is ticking..."

Hannah sighed and slipped back beneath the covers. She'd heard the clock-ticking speech many times before, and she really wasn't in the mood for it that morning.

"Some of your doctor friends are married, aren't they?"

"Yes Mum," Hannah said for the hundredth time. "Some of them are married."

Her mum clucked her tongue. "So, there is no reason for you to still be single. Have you at least been out on a date since we last saw you?"

It was embarrassing that her mother felt she could interfere in her love life to such a level. If she wasn't bothered about being single, why did it have to bother Mum so much?

"Yes, Mum. Look, do we need to discuss this every time you call? How are you? How's Dad?"

She wished her mother would ask about her job when she rang, instead of jumping straight into men and settling down and marriage, but she didn't think she would ever change.

"Your father is desperate to get back to his gardening," Mum said with a sigh. "You know how he is, and he's bored being around the house with the rubbish weather we've been having lately."

"He needs a more all-weather hobby," Hannah said, dragging herself out of bed to put the kettle on. She needed some caffeine in her system.

They chatted for a little while about Mum's church friends and Dad's hearing test, before Hannah wrapped up the conversation.

"I'll see you soon, okay? Next Sunday that I'm off, we'll do lunch."

"I'll believe it when I see it, Hannah. And think about what I said – you need to get out and date, find Mr Right. We just want you to be happy..."

When her mum had finally put the phone down, Hannah manually put the heating on and curled up on the sofa with a blanket and her coffee. She loved her job, but she also loved days like this where she didn't need to be anywhere at all.

There's plenty of time to settle down and have a family, she thought with a sigh – if settling down and having a family was definitely what she wanted, which she wasn't totally sure it was.

She'd worked too hard to get where she was to give it all up because some man she liked came along. And where on earth would kids fit into her punishing schedule of nights and weekends?

She sipped her coffee and flicked the television on. If only her mum could understand that she was happy with her life the way it was – even if it wasn't what her mum would choose.

CHAPTER TWO

Hannah returned home after a long shift, buzzing with adrenaline. There'd been an accident in a local factory, and A&E had been rammed – but they'd managed to treat every single patient without loss of life or limb. She was unbelievably proud of herself and her team, and it would take a while for the high to wear off, even though she'd been working since the early hours of the morning.

Unusually, she'd left the hospital at a completely different time to her friends, and so there was no one to get an early dinner with. So she'd come home, basking in the glow of a successful day of emergency medicine.

She picked up her mail from the mat on the floor and threw it on the table while she ordered a takeaway. She decided on pizza, because it would be quick and easy, and noticed a missed call from her mum as she did so. Twice in one week – she was clearly feeling more neglected than usual.

Not wanting to take the glow off her day, she decided to call her back later, and instead jump in the shower before the pizza arrived.

She sang to herself in the shower, some song that had been on the hospital radio that she couldn't even remember the name of, and changed into soft, long-sleeved pyjamas ready for an easy evening on the sofa. She had a bottle of wine in the fridge, and a film ready on the telly, by the time her pizza arrived.

"Thanks," she said as she took it from the young lad and took it to the kitchen. It smelt amazing, and her rumbling stomach reminded her, as it often did, how long it had been since she had eaten. The pizza was too big for her to eat in one go, but she liked to have leftovers; her fridge was so often empty, and it was nice to come home to something easy to heat up when she'd been working a long shift. And every shift seemed to run long these days. There just seemed to be no money to hire more doctors or nurses, and so they were all constantly pulling overtime. While she loved the job, she didn't love how they were overworked. She could see how doctors were burnt out by the time they were forty – especially if they had other commitments at home.

Luckily, she only had to worry about herself, and whether she was eating and sleeping enough. Which she did try to do... Well, most days.

The film – an action remake that she'd heard was good – wasn't keeping her attention, so she wandered over to collect her mail from the table, leaving it playing in the background. The first two were bills, which already had direct debits set up so didn't need any attention, but the third was more unusual: a handwritten envelope. Hannah couldn't remember the last time she'd got handwritten mail and she tore it open, her curiosity piqued.

Oscar Reynolds and Christi King are delighted to invite you to their wedding on July 14th, at Cove Crest Inn, Hope Cove, Devon. More details to follow.

Hannah hadn't even known her cousin Oscar was seeing

anyone, let alone engaged. She tried to remember the last time she'd spoken to him. It was years, she was sure. She'd just been so busy, and he lived in the middle of nowhere in Devon. She'd promised to go down for a holiday, the last time they'd spoken, she seemed to remember – but when did she get time for a holiday?

They'd got on well as children though, and their families had often gone on holiday together, leaving the two only children to entertain themselves on campsites or beaches or in the woods – wherever they'd chosen that year.

It was nice of him to invite her, considering how they'd not been in touch in years...and yet part of her couldn't help but think of how difficult it would be to get a weekend off, and then to spend that weekend travelling to Devon, where it would surely be the perfect opportunity for her parents to wax lyrical about the benefits of marriage.

She knew she ought to ring her mum back, but with the appearance of the invitation, she was pretty sure what the topic of conversation would be. Instead, she paused the dull film and hit dial on Oscar's number, hoping it hadn't changed in the time since she'd last spoken to him.

"Hello?"

"Hi, Oscar," she said, feeling a little silly for ringing up out of the blue. "It's Hannah...Martin."

"Hannah! I thought it was your number. How are you?"

Hannah smiled at the warmth in his voice, and the way he instantly put her at ease about ringing. He had always been easy to get along with, and it seemed time had not changed that.

"Good, thanks. Busy, you know, but good. But what about you? I just got your beautiful wedding invitation!"

"I'm good," Oscar said. "Busy – we bought an old house and renovated it, it's a B&B now, so I've got that on top of my landscaping work... But I love it."

"And you're getting married..."

"And I'm getting married," he said, and she could hear that he was smiling even though she couldn't see him.

"I'm sorry I haven't been in touch lately. I didn't even know you were seeing anyone..."

Oscar laughed. "I've been just as useless, don't worry. And you have more of an excuse – being a doctor must take up an awful lot of time!"

"It certainly does. So, what's she like?"

"She's a whirlwind," Oscar said. "She came to Devon a couple of years ago, just for the summer, to help on her aunt's campsite... And, well, one thing led to another, and she ended up staying here, we moved in, set up the B&B... and then I proposed."

He sounded so happy that she couldn't bring herself to feel sickened by how in love they clearly were, as she usually did when her friends talked about their partners like that.

"Well, I'm really pleased for you, Oscar. And I can't wait to meet her – and come down to Devon again!" She was very definitely a city girl, but she had visited Devon a few times as a child, and it was certainly picturesque. Perfect for a holiday – although she couldn't imagine living there.

"So you'll come?"

"Of course, I just need to sort it with work."

"Brilliant. If you need a lift from the station or

anything, let me know – Christi was pretty shocked when she got down here at how little public transport there is," he said with a laugh.

"Oh, did she come from a big city?" Hannah asked, intrigued at what could have made her want rural life.

"London," Oscar said with a chuckle. "Just like you."

"Wow. That is...certainly a big change." Privately, she could not imagine giving up city living because of a man – even one as lovely as her cousin Oscar. But of course, she didn't say that. "I'm presuming Mum and Dad will be driving down, so I'll co-ordinate with them – so don't worry about needing to pick me up. You'll be busy enough that weekend, I'm sure!"

"I'm really glad you're coming," Oscar said. "And hopefully Aunt Mary and Uncle John, too."

"I'm sure they'll be delighted," Hannah said, answering on her parents' behalf. They loved a wedding, and she couldn't imagine them missing it.

"Since Dad died last year... I really want to make sure I don't lose touch with family. It's so easy, when you're young and busy, to let it all fall by the wayside..."

"Don't I know it," Hannah said with a sigh. "And I was sorry to hear about Uncle Felix," she added. She'd known of Oscar's father's death, but hadn't thought to send her condolences – something she felt bad about now that she actually thought about it. She was so wrapped up in her work that sometimes she just didn't consider something until it was put right in front of her. She knew her parents had attended the funeral, but it was a day she had been scheduled to work, and she hadn't seen her uncle in so long that she hadn't really thought about trying to move her days.

"Thanks. I'm moving Mum down here too... It's

too far to visit her regularly, and she can't manage the journey. There's a granny flat in the B&B, so she's going to live there. Independence, but we can support her too. Will be a lot less stressful..."

"Wow, that's great," Hannah said. She couldn't imagine anything more stressful than living under the same roof as her mother – granny flat or not. But Oscar clearly had a different relationship with his, and besides, it was easy for Hannah to visit her parents on the outskirts of London whenever she felt like it. Which was probably not as often as she ought to...

But still, it wasn't like travelling the length of England, which was what Oscar had to do to see his.

Hannah decided to return her mother's phone call the following morning, when she didn't have long before she had to get to work – an easy excuse to keep the call brief.

"Hey, Mum," she said as soon as her mum picked up. "Sorry I didn't call back yesterday, work was crazy..."

"Better late than never. I was just wondering, did you get your invitation to you cousin Oscar's wedding?"

Exactly why I thought she'd rung, Hannah thought to herself with a wry smile. "I did."

"And will you be able to go? Your father and I are going to book rooms in the hotel in Hope Cove where the wedding is, and they'll go fast, so we wanted to see if you wanted us to sort one out for you..."

"Yes, I'll make it work. That sounds good, thanks – and can I get a lift down with you, too? I don't think public transport is all that great round there, from what Oscar says."

"Of course, darling. So you've spoken to your cousin? Did he tell you about the proposal?"

Hannah thought back to the conversation they'd had. "No, he didn't mention it," she said. But then she hadn't asked about it, either...

"Such a romantic story," Mum gushed, and Hannah glanced the clock. She was ready for work with her shoes on and her bag on the table, and she'd need to leave in the next twenty minutes if she was going to be on time.

"Was it?" she asked, figuring she'd just have to cut Mum off if the conversation carried on for too long.

"Oh yes. He proposed on the beach, at sunset," she said. "Just the two of them on some beach they had gone to together before they were even dating. Down on one knee, a diamond ring, a bottle of champagne waiting – the whole package."

"That's nice." Hannah didn't know if it was wrong of her, but she'd never dreamed of some perfect proposal, or even of her wedding day, as she knew lots of people did. She assumed it would happen, at some point, but she didn't really have any thoughts about it.

She hoped, if this Christi had been the type to imagine her future proposal, that it was everything she had ever wished for.

"We can't wait to meet her. Oh, and a wedding in Devon...it's just the perfect location! Are you sure you'll want to travel with us? You're not taking a date?"

Hannah sighed. She hadn't even thought about the possibility of needing a plus one. The invitation hadn't said anything about it...but then it has also said there was more information to follow.

"I-" She wished she'd thought of that possibility, so that she had an answer ready. "I'm not sure yet. But whether it's just me, or me plus one – can we travel with you? It will be easier that way."

"Of course, dear. Very romantic places, weddings, you know. The perfect opportunity to really get to know how someone feels about settling down, marriage, kids..."

Sensing the path the conversation was heading down, Hannah decided it was time to cut and run. "I'd better dash Mum, don't want to be late for work. We'll talk soon though, okay?"

CHAPTER THREE

July rolled around in the blink of an eye, and Hannah had barely given the wedding a moment's thought. When the full invitation had arrived, informing her of the time, the gift registry, and that she did indeed have a plus one, her mind had focussed on it for a short while... But then life had got in the way, and suddenly it was the very next weekend.

She did not have the energy to scrounge up a date. There were people she could have asked, but with it being in Devon, she would have had to spend the whole weekend with them, too – and she just felt like it might be easier to just deal with her parents' disappointment and constant comments about her needing to settle down.

Hannah had been so wrapped up in her usual cycle of work, sleep, and time with her friends, that she hadn't even confirmed she could get the weekend off. And there her name was on the rota, for the Saturday night shift... The busiest of the week, and the one that most people wanted off.

But she had promised Oscar she would attend his wedding. She hadn't meant to forget all about getting the time off agreed...time had just disappeared.

She didn't have a dress, or shoes, or a gift either.

She really had dropped the ball.

While to some, the thought of spending a day

shopping for a new dress would be pleasant, to Hannah, it was just another chore that had to be completed.

She lived in scrubs at work and jeans and T-shirts at home. She was not the sort of woman who really wore dresses – and she was quite happy with that. But going to a wedding would require a new dress.

She only had a couple of hours before work to devote to the task, so she chose a street with several shop options and began the dreaded search. Since her mother would certainly criticise her lack of a date, she didn't want to give her anything wardrobe-related to comment on.

Everything in the shops seemed too frilly, too fussy, or too irritating to wear for a full day. She tried on four dresses, but each was worse than the last. She looked at her watch with a sigh. Time was ticking away, and she had to get something today. After all, the wedding was only days away – and she still needed to persuade someone to trade shifts with her.

"Can I help you, madam?" a voice said, and Hannah turned to see a shop assistant with a broad smile and a youthful face. She tried not to bristle at the use of the word 'madam.' Perhaps the girl could find something more quickly than Hannah's own disastrous search.

"I need a dress for a wedding. And shoes, too. I don't normally wear dresses, so anything you can suggest..."

"Of course. Are you in the wedding party?"

Hannah laughed. She wasn't even reliable enough to make sure she had the time off work. She certainly was not in the wedding party. "No... But I am related to the groom, so I guess I'll probably be in some family pictures."

The girl smiled and nodded. "So would you want something fairly simple? Easy to dance in?"

"I doubt I'll do much dancing," Hannah said. She could already picture the scene. The only people she would know, aside from the groom, were her parents. So she supposed she would end up propping up the bar alone. Part of her was tempted to avoid getting the time off, to make her excuses... but that wouldn't be fair. Not so late in the day. "But simple, yes. Nothing that's going to be an issue when I want to sit down... or if I want to run away."

The poor shop assistant looked torn – she clearly wasn't sure whether Hannah meant that as a joke or not.

"I think we have the perfect dress over here," she said, leading Hannah towards the far end of the shop. She pointed out several dresses hanging on the rack, each very similar, but in different colours. Hannah reached out to touch them and was surprised to find the fabric was far softer than it looked, not stiff and unforgiving like the ones she had tried on before. And thankfully, there wasn't a frill in sight.

"They're very simple," the shop assistant said, seeming to take Hannah's reaction as a negative. "But they're very flattering on, I promise. We've sold several for weddings this year."

"I believe you," Hannah said, running her hand across the different colours – black, red, pink, green. "I suppose I should try one on. What colour do you think, for a July wedding?" It was probably a decision she should have made herself, but she had twenty minutes until she needed to leave for work, and she had no idea which colour to choose. The girl's opinion would be far better than her own.

"The pale pink or the mint green, I would say. Both would suit your colouring perfectly."

Hannah smiled. "Excellent. I'll try them on then." She really hoped the girl worked on commission. She was earning every penny.

"If it would help, I could pick out some shoes to match? Save you some time?"

Hannah took the pink and the green dresses and smiled broadly. "I think you must be my guardian angel."

"I'll take your Saturdays for a month," Hannah said, following Duncan around A&E. "I know I should have arranged cover earlier, but you know what it's like – it just crept up on me..."

Duncan sighed. "You know I want to help...and normally, I would. But Theresa is already fed up with the hours I'm working, making it unpredictable when I can have Ellen. If I throw in a sudden Saturday night that she wasn't expecting..."

"What if I ring her, explain you're doing me a huge favour, and do every one of your Saturdays for a month? That way you can promise you'll have Ellen without having to worry about the rota. And I'll dog-sit for you next time you want to go away?"

Duncan scribbled something on the chart in front of her and sighed again. "Is it really urgent?"

Hannah nodded. "A family wedding that I RSVP'd to ages ago. I've even been out buying a dress this morning..."

Duncan laughed. "Wow, you must be serious about going if you went dress shopping. And it would be a shame for you to have tortured yourself like that for it to go to waste."

"Exactly. So will you do it, please?" Hannah begged.

"I don't want to let my cousin down, and I can't bear the thought of the guilt trip my parents will put me through if I say I couldn't get the time off." Another sigh, another scribble on a patient's chart, and then Duncan turned to face her.

"Oh, go on then. But I'm holding you to the month of Saturdays. And the dog-sitting."

"Yes, yes, of course. Thank you, Duncan." She threw her arms around her friend and then scurried off as a buzzer sounded in exam room one.

Well, she had the dress, she had the shoes, and now she had the day off. She supposed she was going to the ball after all.

On Friday afternoon, with her hair still damp from the hurried shower she'd taken after work, Hannah waited outside her flat for her parents. She only had a small holdall for the weekend away, with the new mint green dress folded carefully in it. The angel of a shop assistant had assured her it wouldn't crease – which was good since it would need to be in the bag for several hours, and she wasn't even sure she owned an iron any more. She certainly couldn't remember the last time she'd used it.

Mum and Dad's silver estate pulled up and Hannah hopped in the back, throwing her bag in before her and holding her takeaway coffee carefully in one hand.

"Hey," she greeted her parents, struggling to do the seatbelt while holding her drink.

"Hi, love," Dad said, glancing in the rearview mirror and smiling at her.

"That coffee better not touch the seats, Hannah," Mum said with a frown. "You know I don't like drinks in the car."

"Yes Mum," Hannah said. "I've been up since four, I needed some caffeine."

"Since four?" Dad said, pulling away from the kerb. "You know we've got the rehearsal dinner when we get there, right? You'll be exhausted."

"I'm used to it," Hannah said. "And the wedding's not 'til lunchtime tomorrow, I can catch up with a lie-in."

"You'll need time to get ready though, won't you?" Mum said, and Hannah could feel the disapproving look her mum was giving her damp hair and scruffy jeans.

"You can close your eyes while we drive," Dad said. "It's a long journey."

CHAPTER FOUR

The hotel, she had to admit, was beautiful. Set into the cliff, overlooking the beach and the glittering ocean, she could see the appeal of a wedding here – or even a holiday. Although, it still wasn't enough to make her understand why someone would move here from the city.

She had managed a couple of hours of uncomfortable sleep in the car as Dad drove, which made her feel at least a little more with it. It had also meant she avoided most of her mother's thoughts on the fact that she was attending this wedding without a date.

"It certainly is beautiful," Dad said as he drove into the steep car park and found a space.

"I wonder if they'll have photos on the beach," Mum said. "I do hope the weather is as beautiful as it is today."

"There are people swimming in the sea," Hannah said, a little surprised. The weather was pleasant, but she wouldn't have thought it warm enough for swimming in England.

"Oh, I can see the appeal," Dad said. "I almost wish I'd packed my trunks – although there won't be much time for swimming, I guess. Not with the wedding tomorrow, and us leaving Sunday. When was the last time we went to the seaside, eh, Mary? We should come down again when we can just spend time doing what we want."

"We've just got here, John, you can't be planning for us to come down again immediately."

They checked in, and Hannah was pleased that she had let her mother book the hotel. It would certainly be easier to be in the same place as the wedding, and it really was beautiful. Her room had a sea view, and she spent some time watching the waves crashing onto the shore. There wasn't long before she had to be changed and ready for the rehearsal dinner, and she hurriedly took out the dress for the following day and hung it up, hoping the sales girl had been right and that it wouldn't stay creased – or at least that the creases would fall out.

For that evening, she had only a simple little black dress. She hadn't wanted to buy two new outfits, so she had fallen back on an old standby. She jumped into the shower and tried to remember who was going to be at the dinner. It was nice of Oscar to have invited them, but she doubted she would know anyone there aside from her parents. And even with her nap, she felt like they had exhausted most topics of conversation that didn't involve why Hannah was not yet married, and when they might expect grandchildren.

The rehearsal dinner was in the same hotel, so Hannah made her way down alone, feeling a little self-conscious. The little black dress was her fall-back because it was easy, and she knew it flattered her boyish figure. But she rarely wore dresses, and seldom got dressed up – and she couldn't help but wonder if everyone would be judging her as much as her mother surely would.

She hovered in the doorway of the dining room, hoping to see her parents. She should have arranged to meet them before coming down, she thought. They were judgmental, but at least she knew them.

"Hannah!" a voice called. The smiling figure of her cousin Oscar came over, still as dark-haired as she remembered him, although now with a smattering of dark stubble across his face.

"Oscar! It's so great to see you."

"And you. You look great. Thanks for coming all the way down here."

"I wouldn't have missed it," she said. He didn't need to know how close she had come to not being able to find cover – or not being able to find a dress, for that matter.

"Come, sit down. We've got wine open. I want you to meet everyone – and Christi. I want you to meet Christi especially." Hannah grinned at his enthusiasm. He really was excited to see her, and his happiness was catching.

He led her over to a large table in the middle of the dining room, which also had incredible views of the ocean. Most of the seats were still empty, but a tall, curly-haired brunette figure sat in one, next to an older lady in a dress covered with sunflowers.

"This is Christi," he said, gesturing at the pretty brunette. "And her aunt, Olivia. This is my cousin, Hannah."

Christi stood and reached across the chair for an awkward hug. "Hannah, it's great to meet you. You're the doctor, right?"

Hannah laughed. "That's me!"

Olivia reached across to shake her hand. "Lovely to meet you, dear. And what beautiful weather you've brought with you! Let's hope it stays for tomorrow."

"I don't believe you get miserable summers here," Christi said. "They've always been sunny since I moved here."

"You've just been wearing rose-tinted glasses," her

aunt said with a laugh. Christi gave Oscar a sickeningly in-love smile.

"The forecast is looking good for tomorrow," Hannah said. "I heard it on the radio on the way down here. But I'm sure it will be a lovely day, whatever the weather."

"It will," Oscar agreed. "Sit, sit – let me get you a glass of wine. Everyone else should be here soon. Mum's just in the bathroom, and Christi's family are all staying in the hotel, so they should be down soon."

"Yeah, Mum and Dad are upstairs too." Hannah took a seat and gratefully sipped the glass of wine that Oscar had poured for her. "It's a beautiful hotel. What a great spot to get married."

"We think so," Christi said with a grin. "We love the sea, but getting married on the beach isn't very practical in England! Even though I don't believe it ever rains here in the summer..."

Oscar laughed. "If you've got time on Sunday, I'd love to show you our B&B in Malborough, too. We've got friends staying there for the wedding."

"I'd love to," Hannah said, pleased that things were so easy with Oscar in spite of the years between contact. "I'm not sure what time we've got to leave, though..."

The doors to the restaurant opened, and a large group of men entered, followed by Hannah's mum, dad, and Auntie June – Oscar's mum.

"Time for an influx of Kings," Christi said, sighing slightly as she stood.

Christi looked to Oscar for an explanation.

"Christi's surname is King – for another day, anyway," Oscar said with a laugh. "All her family's here, so I presume her parents aren't far behind. Things aren't always the most...harmonious between them."

"Oh, I can understand that," Hannah said, as her own parents took their seats on the opposite side of the table.

The table soon filled with relatives and friends of both Christi and Ivy, and the wine flowed as easily as the conversation. Hannah found herself seated next to Christi's maid of honour, a woman she thought was probably a couple of years younger than herself, with long brown hair and a handsome blond man on her arm.

"This is Ivy, and Alfie," Christi introduced them. "And this is Hannah, Oscar's cousin."

"Lovely to meet you," Hannah said, shaking both their hands.

"Who did you get to babysit Rose?" Christi asked.

"Dad," Ivy said. "He's great with her – although this is the longest I've ever left her. And I'm sure she'll still be awake when we get back!"

"He spoils her," Alfie said, but he was smiling as he said it.

"Not as much as you do," Christi said with a laugh.

"How old is your daughter?" Hannah asked.

"Coming up to three months," Ivy said. "I wouldn't have left her for anything less important than Christi and Oscar's rehearsal – and she's coming to the wedding with us tomorrow."

Hannah smiled. All she knew about small children came from a medical standpoint, not a parenting one. And she knew the sight of a tiny baby would only prompt her mother on the topic of grandchildren...

"How's remote working?" a dark-haired man across the table called over to Alfie. "Managing with the dire internet speeds down here?"

Alfie laughed. "It's not as bad as you make out. Our new place has pretty decent fibre – I'm managing video calls and everything!"

"Have you recently moved down here?" Hannah asked.

Alfie nodded. "I was down here part-time for a while...but now Rose has been born, Ivy and I have got a place together. I'm working remotely for now, and travelling back up to Oxford when I have to for a case..."

"What do you do?" Hannah asked, finding a topic she was much more comfortable discussing.

"I'm a lawyer," he said. "And I'm not keen on leaving my firm...but the commute isn't feasible in the long run!"

Ivy looked up at him with a broad smile, and he wrapped his arm around her. "We'll figure it out, though."

Hannah wanted to ask why they didn't move to Oxford, but she thought it would sound rude. There obviously was a reason so many people loved Devon. Just because she didn't understand the appeal, didn't mean she ought to be questioning everyone's decisions. After all, some people – people she didn't understand – hated London.

While they ate the meal – perfectly cooked lamb with mint sauce – Hannah listened in to the conversations around her. Christi and Oscar were chatting away with her aunt on the other side about bookings on a campsite. Opposite, the dark-haired man who had spoken to Alfie, and his dark-haired companions, discussed whether an early morning swim in the sea the following day was a good idea. Hannah's parents spoke softly with her Aunt June about her move down to Devon. The couple that Hannah thought were Christi's parents seemed to be having a debate over some legal precedent, and Hannah wondered if they, too were lawyers.

All in all, the meal was a success. Despite not knowing anyone, Hannah felt at ease, and by the end of the evening she was full, tired, and a little tipsy. She said goodnight to her parents, and Oscar and Christi. Alfie and Ivy had bowed out before the coffee, wanting to get home to their baby, and the rest of the guests disappeared to go home or to their hotel rooms.

Hannah knew she ought to go to bed. She hadn't had much sleep the night before, and the wedding would be a long day. But she didn't feel like disappearing to her empty double bed, and so she headed to the bar for a nightcap. Just one, and she thought she could people-watch for a while before heading to bed. Hopefully the wrinkles had fallen from her dress hanging upstairs, otherwise she would have to see if the hotel had an iron she could borrow...

"I'll have a glass of the house white, please," she said to the bartender, giving her room number when he asked. She sat at the bar and looked out towards the sea. Although it was late, it wasn't yet fully dark, and she could still make out the waves and the outline of the rocks. It certainly was beautiful.

"Mind if I join you?"

She turned to find the dark-haired man from the dinner table, the one who had asked Alfie about remote working, standing before her. She gestured to the empty stool beside her. "Feel free. Although I'm not staying long – need to get some sleep before the wedding tomorrow!"

The man laughed and ordered a whisky on the rocks from the bartender, before taking a seat on the stool. His legs reached the floor, unlike hers, and his shiny black shoes rested on the carpet. He had loosened the tie he had been wearing, and he leaned back against the bar.

Hannah wondered whether she ought to ask his name, but then thought she had probably been told it and forgotten, and did not wish to look rude.

"It was a lovely evening," she said instead. "They seem very happy."

"Oh, yes, they really do. Perfect for each other. Soul mates, if you believe in such a thing," he said with a laugh.

"Do you?" she asked.

"I think my brain's too logical to believe in them, although it would certainly make life easier."

Hannah sighed. "Agreed. My parents are so desperate for me to settle down, it would certainly be a lot easier if there was one magic match for me!"

The dark-haired man next to her sipped his whisky. "Ah yes, the parental expectations..."

"You get similar?" she asked.

"They're lawyers, same as me, so you would think they understood the demands. But their expectations are rather high – in all areas."

Hannah rolled her eyes. "Mine haven't got a clue about the pressures of being a doctor. They act as if the only measure of success is being married and having kids by the time you're thirty – so I'm very definitely a failure."

"You're a doctor, then?"

Hannah nodded. "Emergency medicine."

"Definitely not a failure, then," Anthony said. "And no offence to the bride and groom, or any of the other loved-up couples, but I'm not sure settling down is so much of an achievement – more something that happens to you, and you get swept along with it whether you like it or not!"

Hannah laughed. She wished she remembered his name, because he was funny, and clearly shared her outlook on life. She was very happy for Christi and Oscar – but with them, and Alfie and Ivy, looking at each other with love-struck expressions, it was nice to find someone who was a little more cynical about romance.

He finished his whisky and glanced at the clock. "I'd suggest another...but I really should be getting to bed, if I'm going to be up for that early morning swim I promised my brothers."

Hannah laughed. "Rather you than me!"

"It seemed like a good idea at the time... I'm not sure it will at the crack of dawn. But I'll see you tomorrow?"

"I'll see you tomorrow," she said, and his answering smile filled her with warmth.

It was only as he walked away, his dark hair catching the light from the old-fashioned chandeliers in the bar, that she realised she still had no idea what his name was – or how he knew the bride and groom.

CHAPTER FIVE

She might have been cynical about love, but even Hannah could not help but be moved by watching Christi and Oscar getting married. Christi looked beautiful in a princess-style gown with a corset top and delicate sequins all over the lace, which caught the sunlight as she moved. Oscar couldn't keep his eyes off her.

Christi's maid of honour, with her long dark hair plaited down her back, followed her down the aisle and then took the bouquet. She was beautiful, but everyone paled in comparison to the bride.

They'd written their own vows, and as Oscar spoke of the light Christi had brought into his life, Hannah felt a tear come to her eye.

This was ridiculous. She didn't cry at weddings. She didn't cry, full stop. And yet there was something so beautiful about the ceremony, about these two people who had found one another and were promising to spend the rest of their lives loving each other, that made her feel emotional. That made her think maybe it might be something she wanted. One day. When she had more time.

As the new Mr and Mrs Reynolds recessed back down the aisle, broad smiles on their faces, Hannah joined the rest of the congregation, including her parents beside her, in applauding.

"That was beautiful," Mum said on her right-hand side. "Just beautiful. Just imagine, Hannah, one day..."

And there it was. A constant reminder that until she was wed, her parents would view her as a failure.

The ceremony had been beautiful, but while the photos were being taken, Hannah had to endure more comments than she could bear about her single status.

"Look at all this, Hannah. Don't you want this?" her mum had asked after the big family photo.

"If we have a son-in-law, one day..." she had begun while the canapes were being passed around.

"Three grandchildren, Elsa down the road has. Did you know that? And she's five years younger than I am!"

"I get the hint, Mum," Hannah said, taking yet another glass of champagne from the platters that were being circulated. All she'd eaten all day were four tiny canapes, and the champagne was quickly going to her head.

"I'm just saying love, time is ticking. You know how proud we are of your achievements, but don't let your job stop you from settling down. Your job won't be there to keep you company when you retire, I can tell you that."

"I'm going to get some fresh air," Hannah said, standing up and taking the glass of champagne with her.

Outside, she watched the guests mingling in their finest clothes. Christi and Oscar were down on the beach having photographs taken, and the rest of the guests were milling around either inside the hotel, or out on the terrace in the sunshine.

"Hi again," a rich voice said, and Hannah turned to see the handsome, dark-haired man she'd shared a drink with the previous evening. He was wearing a dark suit and a shirt in a shade of purple that complimented the flowers and the maid of honour's dress. Hannah had to admit, if she had thought he was handsome the previous night, it was nothing compared to today.

The man certainly looked good in a suit.

She found she was pleased with the mint green dress she was wearing, that the talented shop assistant had picked out. She felt comfortable in it, but also like she looked her best – and she really wanted to look her best with this handsome as sin man before her.

"Hi," she said with a smile. "Fancy running into you here."

He laughed. "Who would have thought it." He snagged two glasses of champagne from a tray being carried past, and handed her one. She had only just finished her last, but she took it anyway, feeling the bubbles go to her head.

"What a beautiful day," she said, gesturing with her glass of champagne at the bright blue sky and the hot sun. "Did you get your swim?" she asked.

"I did, as it happens. I wasn't sure I would, but once my brothers decide something, there's no backing out."

"Very brave of you," Hannah said. "I never asked you last night – how do you know the –"

"Hannah!" Her mother's voice came across the balcony. "There you are. We've been looking everywhere for you."

Hannah closed her eyes and grimaced. "Sorry," she said to the tall, dark, handsome stranger. "My mother..."

He laughed. "Understood. I'll see you later, I'm sure." And with that, he was gone – and once again, she had not managed to get his name, or how he knew the newlyweds.

"He was very handsome," Mum said in a voice that was far too loud when she got close enough to speak. "Who is he?"

Hannah sighed. "Another wedding guest, Mum," she said, feeling irritated. She had come out here to get away from the constant digs about her single status.

"I'm just asking, dear. Now, they want us to sit down, that's why I came to find you. Did you see the maid of honour's baby? Such a little doll. And she's younger than you, you know?"

Hannah groaned and followed her mother inside, hoping there would be plenty of wine served with the wedding breakfast.

Even after the large meal, Hannah could feel that the alcohol had gone to her head. While the staff were rearranging the dining room for the evening do, she stepped out onto the balcony and took in some deep breaths of fresh, salty air. The air definitely felt different here. She watched the waves reflecting the setting sun as they lazily drew into the shore and then pulled away. All in all, it had been a fun, if exhausting, day so far. It was nice to see her cousin again, and to see him so happy. The food had been great, the alcohol had flowed freely – and that had helped to temper her mother's comments, just a little.

She'd last seen her mother cooing over Ivy's little baby girl, Rose. The baby was cute, certainly – but once you'd seen one baby, you'd seen them all, in Hannah's mind. Maybe it was different when it was your own. If her mother's warnings were anything to go by, she'd never find out.

Most of the guests were sitting chatting, or had gone to their rooms to rest while the evening entertainment was set up. The balcony was fairly empty, and so when she heard footsteps, she turned to see who was joining her.

It was him, again.

She smiled, her head feeling a little fuzzy, and he leant on the balcony beside her. "I'm not following you, I promise."

Hannah laughed. "I'm not sure I believe you."

"I just needed a break. For a minute. Parents, you know..."

Hannah rolled her eyes. "Oh yes, I know."

The evening air was still warm, and the sound of the waves down on the beach filled the silence for a moment.

"Have you seen Hannah?" she heard her mother say. She groaned inwardly, and turned to see her mother talking to Oscar, and apparently searching for her.

Oscar pointed towards the balcony, and Hannah did the only thing she could think to do to avoid yet another onslaught of comments about her single status: she turned to the dark-haired mystery man, pulled him down to her height and pressed her lips to his.

CHAPTER SIX

She didn't think she had ever thought about anything less. One minute she was looking at the waves and enjoying the buzz from the drinks she'd consumed, and the next she was inhaling the woody scent of his aftershave and feeling the warmth of his tall, muscular body pressed against hers. At first he stood as still as a statue, but then he responded, his lips moulding to hers as the waves crashed in the distance behind them.

When she pulled away, Hannah felt the blood rushing to her cheeks. She smiled awkwardly at the handsome, dark-haired man, who looked a little stunned. But he smiled back, and she was relieved he hadn't just dashed away after the impromptu kiss.

Before explaining herself, Hannah turned to look into the dining room of the hotel, which was in the process of being transformed into a place where they could dance. Her mother was nowhere to be seen – so her plan had, at least, been effective.

"Sorry..." she said, turning back to the man. "For jumping on you like that."

He took a sip of his drink. "No need to apologise... Although I admit I'm curious what I said that made me suddenly so irresistible."

Hannah giggled. She was surprised to hear the

sound coming from her mouth; she wasn't one to giggle, normally. But he was funny, and charming, and even a little drunk, she knew he was a very good kisser.

"I hate to be the bearer of bad news, but it wasn't anything you said." She sipped her wine. "My mother was looking for me... I'm just so sick of being asked why I didn't bring a date, why I haven't settled down, when I'm going to give them grandkids..." She sighed. "I just thought it would shut her up to see me with someone. Sorry, I shouldn't have used you like that."

He smiled a warm, broad smile that she was surprised to find sent her pulse skittering. *Must be all the booze*, she told herself.

"I'm not complaining about being used," he said. "And if I can get your parents off your back, I'm happy to help."

"Thank you–" She realised then that she still didn't know his name. "Sorry, I really shouldn't have kissed you when I don't even know your name. Blame the champagne..."

He offered his hand and she shook it, his warm hand dwarfing hers. "Anthony. Anthony King. It's a pleasure to meet you, officially–"

"Hannah," she replied, her brain joining the dots. "Anthony King...so you're related to Christi?"

"I am indeed. Her older brother – well, one of them."

Hannah inwardly groaned. It probably wasn't the best decision to choose the brother of the bride in her spur-of-the-moment ruse. He wasn't exactly someone her parents would forget... But it was too late to worry about that now.

"And you're Oscar's cousin, is that right?"

She nodded; he'd clearly been paying far more

attention to the guests than she had. She'd certainly noticed him – at the rehearsal dinner, at the bar the previous night, outside earlier that day... But she'd not realised he was the bride's brother. It made sense though; the group of handsome men at the rehearsal dinner were clearly all related.

"How many King brothers are there?"

"Worried you've picked the wrong one for your game of pretend?" he asked.

She laughed. "No, just being nosy. And realising I really don't pay enough attention." The wine was making her tongue looser than it probably should be, but she couldn't stop smiling. This was *fun*.

"There's three of us, and then Christi."

"Poor Christi!"

"She would probably agree with you. Mark, the eldest, lives in California, so it's the first time we've all been together in a long time. So she doesn't always have to put up with all of us."

"So, four children, your sister married – are your parents as insistent as mine that you should be settling down and carrying on the family line?" Suddenly, she put a hand to her mouth and swore. "Or are you already married? I just kissed you without even asking, sorry, I–"

"Relax," he said, putting a hand on her shoulder. "I'm a perpetual bachelor, much to my parents' chagrin, so you've done nothing wrong. And yes, they are very confused as to why we can't manage to have glittering careers as well as producing a huge brood of kids, just like they did."

"So the parental disappointment is universal," she said, finding she was rather pleased he wasn't married – and not just because it meant there was no chance of an irate wife coming over to throw a drink at her for touching her husband.

"Indeed. You're a doctor, that was what you said last night, wasn't it?"

Hannah nodded.

"My brother Logan's a doctor, up in Manchester."

"Oh? What's his speciality?"

"Pediatrics," Anthony said. "And he regularly gets the 'when are you going to settle down and find a wife' conversation, so it's not solely for the fairer sex."

"Glad to hear it."

"In fact..." He glanced through the glass doors, where the band was just setting up. "Perhaps we could avoid that conversation for a while from both of our parents."

"Oh?" Hannah raised her eyebrows.

"We could carry on playing pretend for the rest of the night. If they see us together, they'll not have any criticisms, surely?"

Hannah mulled the idea over. It would certainly make the journey home less painful if her mother wasn't just repeating the same old tired lines about biological clocks and time ticking.

She enjoyed his company – so why not pretend there was something more between them for the evening?

"Unless you think you'd prefer the medical King brother, rather than the lawyer," he said with a shrug. "I realise I was just in the right place at the right time..."

"I'm perfectly happy with the King brother I ended up with," she said. "Let's do it. Give them something else to go on about tomorrow."

He offered her his arm. "Excellent. Then can I escort

you to the bar? I think we're in need of another drink..."

For the rest of the evening, she didn't leave Anthony's side. She saw the looks they got from his brothers, his sister, her cousin, and both their parents, as they danced together, getting closer and closer as they imbibed more and more. She couldn't remember when she'd last had so much fun.

At one point, she ended up around a table with the four King siblings and Oscar, as a large tray of shots was ordered.

"To Christi!" one brother – she thought it was Mark – cried, raising a shot in the air and downing it, and encouraging them all to do the same. The tequila was bitter on her tongue, but it slid down easily.

"To Oscar!" another brother said, raising a second shot. "For putting up with her!"

Christi smacked his arm, but they all did the second shot regardless, laughing and spluttering, their eyes watering from the burn of the alcohol.

"Hannah?"

Hannah turned from the group to see her mother and father looking on, bemused.

"Sorry, were you looking for me again?" Hannah asked, stepping away from the crowd.

"Just to say goodnight."

Hannah glanced at the clock and realised it was already approaching ten. The evening had disappeared in a whirlwind of laughter, dancing, and drinks.

"I didn't realise how late it was!"

"Past our bedtime," Dad said with a laugh.

"You seem to be having fun," Mum said, with a

pointed glance at Anthony, who wasn't far behind.

"Yeah," Hannah said with a grin. "It's a great wedding."

"Well, we'll see you at breakfast tomorrow, darling," Dad said, leaning in to kiss her cheek. "Don't drink too much!"

Hannah rolled her eyes, feeling sixteen again, and turned back to the group. There was still another hour before the wedding would come to a close, and she was having far too much fun to go to bed.

"I love this song!" Christi cried, putting down her shot glass and grabbing her new husband by the hand. "Come on, everyone onto the dance floor!"

Hannah didn't recognise the song, but she followed suit, as did all of Christi's brothers, her maid of honour Ivy, and her partner Alfie. Most of the remaining guests joined them as they danced to the beat, and when Anthony took her hand a twirled her around, she just laughed.

Her parents had gone to bed – but Anthony's were the parents of the bride, and they looked like they were going to stay until the end, although they hadn't joined the group on the dance floor. So even if they no longer needed to pretend for her parents, the point of the ruse was to get *both* sets of parents off their backs.

Besides, she was having a good time pretending.

The song changed to a slower ballad, and most of the dancers left to find their drinks. Christi and Oscar slow danced in the centre of the dance floor, looking sickeningly happy. Hannah watched them for a moment, the lights from the projector casting sparkles all around them. Then she turned to leave the dance floor, but Anthony reached out and took her hand, pulling her back.

"Let's dance," he said.

She felt a fluttering in her stomach that had to be from the alcohol, but she didn't let go of his hand. Instead, she swayed with him to the slow music, his hand on her waist. She had no idea how to dance to music like this, and so she let him take the lead, hoping their show was believable. He seemed like a very nice guy, and if both their sets of parents stopped asking questions for a week or two because they'd seen them together, then she would be pleased.

"I've had fun tonight," he murmured, his deep voice close to her ear sending a shiver down her spine that she had not expected. But she smiled, and kept dancing.

"Me too," she said truthfully. "Thanks for playing along..."

"My pleasure."

When she glanced up at him, his dark brown eyes seemed to be smouldering, and he lowered his lips to hers right there on the dance floor.

Alcohol and desire burned through Hannah's veins, and she wrapped her arms around his neck, forgetting they had an audience, forgetting that they were pretending.

When Anthony pulled away, she felt a little breathless, and his eyes seemed to sparkle in the low light.

It was all pretend, of course. But in that moment, it didn't feel so fake.

At eleven o'clock, when the lights were flicked back on and the evening had to come to a close, Hannah felt as though she was floating. She couldn't remember the last time she had so much fun – especially at a family event, and one where her parents had been in attendance.

She took the lift up to the third floor with Anthony and his brothers. They wolf-whistled when he gave her a brief kiss goodnight, keeping up the charade until the very end, before continuing up to the fourth floor where her room was.

She whistled as she strolled down the stripy-carpeted hallway and let herself into her room. She'd thought this weekend was going to be a chore, and it had ended up being anything but.

CHAPTER SEVEN

The next morning, Hannah was not feeling so high on life. The amount of alcohol she had put away became apparent when she woke up with a thumping headache, which was not helped by the thumping on her bedroom door.

She threw on the hotel's robe, since she'd gone to sleep in just her underwear, and pulled open the door to find her mother on the other side, looking irritatingly perky.

"Are you not up yet? Goodness me," Mum said. "We're going down to breakfast. Everyone's eating together, you know, so you'd better get yourself ready to come down quickly. Do you need me to help you pack?"

Hannah groaned at the onslaught of words and information, so soon after she'd woken up.

"Oh, unless you have...*company.*" Mum raised her eyebrows.

"No, Mum, I do not need your help, and I do not have company. I'll meet you down at breakfast."

She jumped into the shower, knowing if she didn't do so straight away, she'd end up falling back to sleep, and scrubbed the remains of the make-up off her face. She didn't have anything fancy packed to wear for the breakfast, and so she hoped her mum wasn't going to have too much to say on her choice of jeans and a T-shirt.

Hair still damp and head still throbbing, she hurried down the stairs, hoping a cooked breakfast would settle her stomach. She had really drunk more than she'd realised at the time. Everything had been so fun in the moment – but now she was paying for it.

Their table was obvious when she went into the dining room, which had been transformed once again from the party venue of the previous evening to a tranquil eating space, overlooking the sea. While there were a few other diners, the majority were at a large central table, which was already nearly full.

There was one space left – and it was next to Anthony.

She smiled and slipped into it, wondering if things would be awkward after their pretend kisses of the previous night.

"Morning," Hannah said to the assembled group, and to Anthony in particular. Several people paused in their conversations to wish her good morning, and then Anthony pulled the pot of coffee towards them.

"Coffee?"

"Please," Hannah said, turning over the coffee cup in front of her, grateful as he poured the strong black liquid into it. "Are you feeling as rough as I am?" she asked, glancing up at him as she picked up the coffee, hoping that drinking it black would help her feel better quicker. Damn, but he didn't look rough at all. Whereas she hadn't even bothered to reapply her makeup after scrubbing off what was left from the night before. She was sure she looked just as terrible as she felt.

"Oh yes," Anthony said with a laugh. "It's been a long time since I drank that much – and it'll be a long time before I do it again."

Hannah nodded. "Agreed. It was a good night though..."

"Yeah," Anthony said instantly. "It really was."

Hannah smiled to herself as she ordered breakfast and listened in on the chat around the table. There were a few crude jokes directed at Oscar and Christi about their wedding night, and the two saps in the centre of proceedings blushed but looked very happy.

Outside, the sun was shining, and the waves lapped lazily against the shore. It really was beautiful, and Hannah had a sudden desire to be outside for a little while, before she had to spend hours in a car with her parents again.

Although the fried breakfast definitely helped the hangover, the thought of sitting in a car for hours made her stomach roll.

"Excuse me," she said as the waiting staff cleared away the plates. "I'm just going to get some fresh air."

She didn't think anyone had particularly noticed her departure, but as she stood on the balcony, leaning against the glass and watching the waves, she heard footsteps behind her.

She turned to find her cousin standing in the doorway. "I just want to thank you for coming again. I know you've got to head off fairly soon..."

Hannah nodded. "Yeah – I've got work first thing tomorrow, so I've got to get back. Sorry I couldn't see your B&B – but maybe next time, yeah?"

Oscar nodded. "Definitely next time. Let's not leave it so long."

"We won't. Thank you for inviting me – and congratulations again. It really was a beautiful day."

Oscar shielded his eyes from the sun, and his grin

widened. "It was everything we hoped it would be. All our friends and family together, a great time, beautiful views – it was perfect."

"It was," Hannah agreed. "Now I just need to get rid of this hangover, and today would be looking up."

Oscar laughed. "Yeah, we got through a fair bit last night. And you and Anthony looked close..."

Hannah blushed. What a ridiculous reaction. She wasn't a teenage girl – and the whole thing with Anthony had been a façade anyway, to get their parents off their backs. Not that she could say that to Oscar...

"He's a nice guy," she said truthfully.

"Yeah, he is. Christi didn't see much of her brothers, for a while – well, I think that was down to how their parents treated her brothers compared to her. But that's another story. Anthony's been down a fair few times now, and he's a decent guy."

Hannah nodded, not sure what else to say. She didn't want to embroil herself in lies. There was no need to fool Oscar, after all – but she couldn't out their ruse.

"I'd better get back in – but we'll see each other soon, yeah?"

They embraced, and Oscar disappeared back inside to his new wife. Hannah vowed to make sure their relationship didn't wither away. It was nice to have family around – well, when they weren't criticising you. She got on with Oscar. It would be a shame not to see him again for several years.

She turned again to watch the waves, and when she heard footsteps once more on the concrete behind her, she presumed it was her parents, telling her it was time to go – or that she was being rude by staying outside. But in truth, the deep lungfuls of sea air were doing more for her hangover than the meal inside had.

"I hope you're not out here avoiding me..."

Hannah whirled around in surprise and felt her cheeks redden yet again at the sight of Anthony. "What? No! Just trying to recover from the hangover, you know..."

He joined her, leaning against the glass. "That's good. I was worried you were regretting our ruse last night, or thought it went too far..."

That drunken kiss on the dance floor came instantly to Hannah's mind, and she shook her head. If he'd been taking it too far, then she'd been right there alongside him. "No, not at all. Just a hangover, honest."

"Good. Because I was wondering what you thought of extending the ruse a little longer..."

Hannah raised an eyebrow. She didn't know if the after-effects of the alcohol were making her slow, but she couldn't think of any reason they would need to prolong their pretend attachment. After all, she was leaving in an hour or so. "Oh?"

"I know you're a very busy woman. And believe me, my schedule is pretty packed. But there are a few family functions coming up that would be a lot easier if I turned up with a date, and not someone who expects more from me – and not someone my parents won't terrify with their grilling... And I thought, perhaps, there might be events like that for you too. A pretend date that you could call on for any family events that need someone to stop the parental nagging..."

Hannah tipped her head to one side, considering his proposal. She didn't enjoy family functions, as a rule – but then, that was most probably because she was usually being nagged about why she didn't have a date. If she had someone – a 'boyfriend' for all intents and purposes – to bring along, it would surely make them more tolerable. And because it was all pretend, there would be no effort needed in between family functions. Just a ready-made date, who would make her look good to her family, and not expect anything more...

"I can see the appeal..." she said slowly. "But my schedule is pretty full on. I need a fair amount of warning to get weekend days off..." That had always been an issue in any real relationship she had. If she dated non-doctors, they didn't seem to understand that she couldn't book weekends off at a moment's notice. And if she dated doctors...well, then neither of them managed to get time off together.

"Understood," Anthony said with a nod. "I'm busy too. We give each other...what, say a month's notice? Nothing that involves too much travel. You're in London, right? So that's pretty central. My parents are in Edinburgh, and then there are events down here, which I'm guessing might become more frequent." He glanced in at the happy bride and groom. "You know, christenings, for example."

Hannah nodded, the idea sounding more and more appealing. "Okay, let's give it a go. And if it's too much for either one of us, we can just cancel the arrangement – no hard feelings, right?"

Anthony held out his hand to shake hers. "Agreed."

The journey home was filled with questions about Anthony, but they were preferable to laments about her single status. Her parents both thought he was a fine young man, with her mother commenting on how handsome he was, and her father noting how stable the income of a lawyer was.

Not that that really mattered. After all, it was a

fake relationship – not that they knew that. And Hannah made a stable enough income of her own. She didn't need to rely on anyone else.

But still, it made a welcome change, and although she did suffer a few waves of nausea thanks to the hangover, she only slept for about an hour, not feeling the need to fake a long sleep to escape her parents' interrogations.

This plan of hers, and the extension of it by Anthony, was going to work out very nicely indeed.

CHAPTER EIGHT

The wedding had seemed like a moment out of somebody else's life. A brief time when she hadn't been thinking about work, and she'd enjoyed being dressed up and socialising with people she'd never met before.

But by Monday afternoon, she was back in the thick of work, and was quite happy to think of nothing else. She loved the hustle and bustle of the hospital, and she thrived on the adrenaline of it all. While her mind did occasionally wander back to that fun night and Anthony, she didn't really dwell on it. They'd exchanged numbers, and if he wanted to carry on with the arrangement as he'd suggested, she presumed he would be in touch when the next family event came up – or she could contact him, she supposed, if something was arranged on her side first.

"Dinner tonight?" Jasmine called as they passed each other in the hallway.

"Sounds good. I'm off at six, if all goes to plan."

"I'm half six, so I'll meet you there, if you get off on time!"

They both knew there was a decent chance Hannah would get sucked into some case right near when she was meant to be leaving, and not be on time anyway. But that was always likely, and there were never any hard feelings between the group if one of them was late or didn't show up altogether.

Something else that was simpler about being single – not needing to worry about upsetting someone waiting at home.

Dinner was fun, although they had questions about the wedding, and she found herself blushing when she talked about Anthony. He was very handsome, and that kiss on the dance floor was still burnt on her brain, even with all the alcohol they'd drunk before and after. They stayed out late chatting and laughing, until the ones with partners at home peeled off to see their significant others, and those without thought it was time for bed.

Hannah thought when she got home after dinner that night that it might be nice to have someone waiting. Not someone who would be irritated with her for being late, but someone who might ask about her day, start dinner, have the heating on in the winter.

Perhaps the next time one of her friends tried to set her up, she'd go along with it – just to see who was out there.

In the end, it was Hannah who ended up contacting Anthony first. Three weeks after the wedding, her parents announced that they had decided to throw a party for their ruby wedding anniversary the following month – and since they had loved Devon so much, they had decided to hold it there.

"You'll be able to get the time off, won't you?" Mum asked.

Hannah bit her lip. It was another weekend – and they were always more of a challenge. But if she said no, then she would immediately win the worst daughter in the world award.

"I'll try to figure it out, Mum," she said, trying to

work out in her head whether she would normally be working that weekend, and if she was, who she could bribe to swap this time.

"Marvellous," Mum said, as though it were already a done deal. "We've booked a beautiful function room in a hotel in Thurlestone – it's overlooking the beach, not too far from where Oliver and Christi's wedding was."

"That sounds nice, Mum."

Forty years of marriage. It was hard to comprehend being married to someone for that long. Longer than Hannah had been alive. She was pleased her parents were still happy, and that they wanted to celebrate. If only it didn't have to be so far away!

"Do you want us to organise a room for you?" Mum asked. "We're going to stay in the hotel. It's not cheap, but I know that's not a huge issue..."

"Let me get back to you," Hannah said, her mind whirring into action. She didn't want a room booking if she couldn't get out of work, for one. And secondly, she needed to get in touch with Anthony. After all, that was the point of this arrangement – to not have to go to family events like these solo, and deal with the ensuing opinions.

"And will you be alone?"

"I–" She hesitated. If she said no, and then Anthony couldn't make it, she would never hear the end of it. But how nice it would be to say that she had a date...

"We understand, darling, but it would be lovely if you could bring someone. Have you been seeing anyone lately?"

They hadn't mentioned Anthony since shortly after the wedding, and it irrationally irritated Hannah that they just assumed it had led nowhere.

"I imagine Anthony will be coming with me, but I'll

need to check his schedule," she said, the words spilling from her mouth. At least if he couldn't come, she could blame his work. Not that she thought her parents would believe her...

"Oh!" Mum said, and Hannah could practically hear her eyes lighting up. "You've been seeing him, since the wedding, have you?"

"Not much in person, what with work, but yeah, we've kept in touch."

"Well, that's exciting, isn't it," Mum said. "A lawyer, too! Fancy that."

Hannah rolled her eyes, but managed to contain her sigh. How was it that her mother could get so excited about someone else's career success – and, notably, a man's – and yet be so unaware of her own daughter's achievements? Was being a doctor really not important, unless she managed to become a wife and mother in a timely manner too?

She felt like she was living in the fifties.

"I presume Oscar and Christi will be invited?"

"Yes, of course," Mum said. "One of the reasons for us having it down there – along with how much we love it – is so that it's easy for your aunt June to be there. You know she can't travel much any more, and now that she's moved to Devon to be near Oscar, it seemed to make the most sense!"

"Great," Hannah said, trying to stir up a little enthusiasm. It would mean finding another dress, she thought with an inward sigh, as well as figuring out the time off. She glanced at the clock. "Sorry, Mum, I've got to dash, I'm in work soon. I'll let you know about the room, yeah?"

"And make sure you confirm with Anthony!"

"Will do, Mum. Bye," she said, knowing Anthony was the very next person she needed to contact. She hoped he'd been serious about the arrangement, and that he was free on that August weekend – because she really did not want to turn up to the party alone.

She felt awkward ringing him, so she typed out a text message, rereading it three times before dithering over the send button.

Hey, it's Hannah, from the wedding. My parents are having an anniversary party on August 30th, in Devon. I wondered if you were free to go... Let me know!

She questioned whether she ought to mention that if he'd changed his mind it was fine, or remind him more who she was, or add a kiss on the end, but she decided against it. The message would end up reading like an essay. She didn't want it to be obvious how nervous she was to ask him about this arrangement. It had been his idea in the first place – but it really would have made her feel better if he'd had to ask her about a family event first. Set the protocol for this weird set-up.

Her phone beeped and her heart raced, but it was just a message from Mum.

Forgot to tell you that the theme is black and silver! So wear black or silver, please – and not the same black dress you pull out for every event!

Why did Mum always have to include some jibe? Hannah had already planned to buy a new dress for the event. In fact, she was thinking that she would head down to the dress shop where she'd so successfully bought the green dress for the wedding, and see if the shop assistant who'd been working the last time was there. She would surely be able to pick out something great in black or silver, without Hannah having to think about it.

Her phone buzzed again, and she expected it to be Mum, adding more information – but it was, in fact, Anthony.

Hey Hannah. Great to hear from you! Yes I can do that weekend. Any specific dress code? I was also going to ask if you could come to my dad's 70th in September, in Edinburgh – it's on a Friday night. X

A smile spread over her face. Just like that, he'd said yes, and her nerves had abated. She quickly replied, before realising she was actually close to being late for work, and hurrying to get ready.

Great! Black and silver is the theme, and fairly smart – so I'd say black suit! Happy to come to your dad's 70th, just give me the date and I'll figure it out with work. She added a smiley face on the end, even though he'd added a kiss, because she didn't want him thinking she expected anything, and then pushed the party and Anthony to the back of her mind, until it came time to shop for a dress.

CHAPTER NINE

"Can I help you, madam?" a tall, dark-haired woman asked as she looked around the dress shop. Hannah couldn't see the assistant who had helped her before. She supposed anyone would do, though she'd made it just so easy...

"There was an assistant who helped me last time I was here..." she said, sure the woman would think she was being ridiculous. "She was small, had red hair... I was just wondering if she was working because she was so helpful last time."

The girl considered her for a moment. "I think you mean Alice. She's on her lunch break at the minute, but she'll be back soon if you want to wait. Or I can help you if you like."

Hannah didn't want to be rude, but she really did want the help of the girl who was apparently called Alice.

"I'll wait, if that's okay," she said with a smile.

The woman looked a little put out but did not argue, and Hannah was left to her own devices. She was never very comfortable in clothes shops. Buying clothes just wasn't something she was particularly interested in – so she always felt inferior around women who seemed to know exactly what to wear to make themselves look good. It was ridiculous, really – she had plenty of skills that those women didn't, after all. But perhaps because her mother always had an opinion on what she wore,

Hannah felt particularly self-conscious in such places.

Thankfully, she hadn't been looking long when Alice appeared – and Hannah was relieved to see that she was the assistant she'd been hoping for.

"Hello again," Alice said with a beam. "Helene said you were looking for me. I hope you haven't been waiting long."

Hannah shook her head. "Oh no, not long at all. It's just that I have another event to go to, and you were so helpful last time, I was hoping you might be able to choose something for me again..." She felt a little ridiculous. A woman in her thirties should surely be able to pick a dress without needing help. But Alice simply smiled and ushered her towards the far end of the shop.

"So, the green dress worked out well for the wedding?"

Hannah nodded. "It was perfect. This time it's my parents' fortieth wedding anniversary. The dress has to be black or silver – but if there's something quite simple again, that doesn't need ironing and isn't complicated to get on and off...that would be brilliant."

Alice's eyes lit up. "Oh, we just got in something beautiful in silver. Just wait there a second..."

She disappeared into the rows of dresses and returned with a metallic silver number, with thin straps and a plunging neckline.

Hannah looked at it doubtfully.

"Now, I know it's a little dressier than the last one. But there are no ruffles, and it's super soft. And it's looked great on everyone I've seen try it on so far!"

Hannah reached for the dress. "I'll give it a go..." she said sceptically, taking it and heading for the fitting room.

She had stripped to her underwear, and was lamenting the fact that she was sure she had no suitable bra to wear with such a neckline, when her phone started to ring. Worried in case it was work, she scrambled around in her bag and found it before it rang off.

"Hello?" she said, not even having looked at the number.

"Hi, Hannah." She was surprised to hear the smooth, deep voice at the end of the line, and found herself clutching the silver dress to her body to cover up, even though of course he couldn't see her.

"It's Anthony," he said, when she didn't say anything. "From the wedding..."

She was almost embarrassed to admit that she'd recognised his voice as soon as he'd spoken.

"Hi, Anthony," she said, hoping she sounded breezy and not as though she was nearly naked in a changing room. "How are you?"

"Great, thanks. Sorry to bother you, are you working?"

"Not this morning," she said.

"I just wanted to run something past you. My friend Alfie – do you remember him, from the wedding? He's with Ivy, who was maid of honour..."

"I remember."

"Well, his parents have a holiday home in Hope Cove. It's empty at the end of August, and he offered it, if we want to stay in it for your parents' party? I didn't know if you already had plans. It's got multiple bedrooms, don't worry..."

She blushed at the implication. "I wasn't worried," she said quickly, before realising that wasn't really necessary to say. "That sounds great, actually. My parents are staying in the hotel, but it's more believable if we're together somewhere!"

"That's what I thought," Anthony said with a deep chuckle. "I thought I'd drive down Saturday morning. I can pick you up, if you like? Unless you planned to travel with your parents..."

"Any excuse not to sit in a confined space with them for several hours is great," she said, then wondered if that made her look bad. "You know, I love them, but close proximity can be a bit much..."

"Oh, I get that. My parents wanted me to join their law firm, up in Edinburgh – they were offended when I declined, but I didn't think working together would be good for our relationship!"

After arranging a time for Anthony to pick her up, and promising to send her address, they hung up, and Hannah finally slipped the dress on.

It was lower cut than she was used to wearing, but the neckline was narrow so didn't feel too exposing. The metallic fabric was cool against her skin, and it did skim the few curves she had nicely, making her feel more feminine than she usually did. She turned, looking at it from all angles, and tried to decide whether she dared to wear it. She had to admit, it did look good...but it was a little out of her comfort zone.

Pulling open the curtain, she saw Alice hovering nearby, organising a shelf of jumpers. When she saw Hannah, she hurried over, a smile on her face. "Wow, that definitely suits you."

"You think?"

"You don't? It's incredible!"

Hannah couldn't help but smile. "It's not what I would usually wear..."

"Isn't it nice to show a different side, sometimes?"

Hannah considered that. It would be nice to surprise her parents by dressing to impress and showing up with a man, for once. And she rather wanted to see Anthony's reaction to the dress. She knew they weren't really dating, but it was nice to feel attractive. And there had definitely been something in that drunken kiss on the dance floor...

"Yes," she said suddenly. "I suppose it is. If you think it looks all right..."

"It looks like it's made for you."

Hannah grinned. "Okay, I'll take it. And could you help me pick some shoes that go with it again?"

"Of course I can."

"You should be a personal shopper you know!" Hannah said, following Alice and feeling lighter now that the task was complete. She just needed to make sure she could get the weekend off, and everything was sorted.

She was pleased that, by the following day, she could ring her mother and tell her everything was indeed sorted.

"Anthony will be coming, Mum," she told her, smiling as she did so. "And we're going to stay in his friend's holiday home, so no need to worry about sorting me a room."

"Well that sounds marvellous. And the time off wasn't a problem?"

Hannah wasn't sure what her mum would have said if it had been an issue, but thankfully it had all been rather simple.

"No, I happened not to be on the rota on the Saturday, and I'm doing a night shift Sunday, so it will work perfectly."

Her nerves about the event didn't reappear until early on the Saturday morning at the end of August, when she was waiting outside her flat for Anthony. It only really dawned on her then how much time she would be spending alone with this man she barely knew. They'd definitely had a good time at the wedding, but there had been plenty of alcohol involved. This time, they would be stone-cold sober, and stuck together in a car for hours, and then a holiday home overnight.

Had she made a terrible mistake, suggesting this?

By the time he pulled up in a shiny red sports car, she was on the brink of cancelling the whole thing. But then he got out, a broad smile on his face, and she calmed down a little.

He was a nice guy. This would be good. Her parents would appreciate her being at their party, and she didn't have to spend the weekend hearing about what a shame it was that she was single.

"Morning," he said, opening the passenger door for you. "Have you been waiting long?"

She shook her head, even though she had made sure she was downstairs early to make things as simple as possible for him.

"I didn't want you to struggle to pull up somewhere, it can be pretty busy."

Anthony nodded. "I must admit, I don't drive into the city often. We just get the train if we come in for work, or drinks."

"Sorry..."

"It's not a problem. Here, let me put your bag in the boot. Do you mind if we stop and get coffee on the way? I was working late last night and could do with the caffeine!"

Hannah slid into the black leather seat, and Anthony closed the door before heading back to the driver's side. "That's fine," she said as she fastened her seatbelt. "I worked late too – I always need coffee!"

After getting coffees at the drive-thru down the road, they set off towards Devon. The radio played in the background, and Hannah soon felt herself relaxing.

"Thanks for agreeing to this," she said, sipping her latte as the car sped down the motorway. "My mother was overjoyed..."

Anthony laughed. "I live to please! Mine was pretty thrilled when I told her I was bringing you to Dad's seventieth next month."

"They might not be so pleased once they get to know me," Hannah said with a shrug. "I'm not sure I'm the type parents fall head over heels for. Unlike you – you smile at my mum and she thinks you're the ideal man!"

"I think you're being too harsh on yourself," Anthony said, reaching for his coffee as Hannah put hers back in the cup holder. Their fingers brushed, and Hannah was surprised at the warmth that spread through her from that brief contact. Perhaps her hand was under a heating vent. The car had a million controls. She had passed her test when she was seventeen, but hadn't needed to drive in years – and had certainly never driven anything quite in this league. She didn't think she'd know where to start. "You're successful, intelligent, pretty – what is there for parents not to love?"

Hannah felt herself blushing, and looked out of her window at the car they were overtaking. She didn't want him seeing her reacting like a schoolgirl to being called pretty.

"Maybe tell my parents that," she said with a self-deprecating chuckle.

"Maybe I will. Surely they realise what an achievement it is, being a doctor in a busy London accident and emergency department?"

Hannah couldn't help but smile. How nice it was to feel truly seen.

"So what were you working on late last night?" she asked, changing the subject a little.

"I'm in family law," he told her. "And I'm currently representing a man in a pretty high-stakes divorce. It could all become public at any time... Anyway, he changed his mind about what he wanted late last night, so we had to go over all the documents again before meeting again with his wife's lawyer Monday."

"Does it put you off marriage, seeing divorces all the time?" she asked, curious.

"Eh..." He paused for a moment. "I don't normally admit this to women," he said with a chuckle. "But since things between us are different... Yes, it does a bit. Makes me wary, at least. I'd want everything legally in place, prenups, agreements over custody of any children, before I'd agree to marry. Which is all very unromantic, I know... But I've seen how badly things can go wrong when nothing was thought through in the first flushes of love."

"That makes sense," Hannah said. "You just want to be prepared. Keep a level head."

"That doesn't always go down too well with women I've dated, though," he said. "Hence the lack of long-term relationships, I suppose – and my mother's eternal disappointment in me."

"I can certainly understand that."

CHAPTER TEN

By the time they arrived in Hope Cove, at the holiday home overlooking the ocean that belonged to Alfie's parents, Hannah's legs felt cramped from sitting in the same position for so long. They'd made good time, and had a few hours to shower, change and mentally prepare before they needed to be at the hotel for the anniversary party.

Did you get to Devon ok? x Mum texted not long after they'd pulled up, and she fired off a quick text to let her know that they had and would see them later.

"Wow, this place is pretty special," Hannah said, following Anthony in. He was carrying both of their bags, and he put them down on the stairs before heading into the living room.

The floor to ceiling windows let in the late summer sunshine, as well as giving amazing views of the beach. It felt like the house was practically on the beach, and Hannah was sure the place had cost Alfie's parents a fortune.

"Do Alfie's parents come down a lot?" she asked.

"I think it was only going to be two, three times a year, when they planned it," he said, wandering over to the open-plan kitchen and setting the coffee machine up. He clearly liked his caffeine as much as Hannah did. "But they sent Alfie down to find somewhere, close the deal for them... Then he met Ivy. And the rest, as they say, is history."

"He's moved down here now, permanently?"

"Pretty much," Anthony replied, searching in the cupboards for mugs. "What with baby Rose, and things between him and Ivy becoming more serious..."

"I can't imagine giving up my life and moving down to the middle of nowhere," she said, watching the waves hitting the shore.

"Me neither. It's lovely down here, but I like living in a city. We were pretty shocked when Christi decided to leave London and move in with Aunt Olivia in Salcombe. She'd always been such a city girl!"

"How did that go down with your parents?" Hannah asked, running a hand over the glossy magazines on the coffee table, depicting the beautiful scenery of the area. The house was like a show home, and she wondered when it had last been used. Or perhaps they just had a really good cleaner.

"As you might expect," he said with a sharp laugh. "They've always been pretty hard on Christi, especially because she didn't go into the sort of career they wanted for her... They thought she was throwing her life away."

"But she clearly didn't think she was..."

Anthony took her head. "She's got a good eye for advertising and marketing, it seems. She turned Aunt Olivia's campsite into a must-stay place, and now this B&B of theirs is always booked up. And of course, she's achieved the one thing that none of the rest of us have – marriage."

"Ah yes," Hannah said with a soft smile. "The holy grail."

"And if she and Oscar decide to have kids... Well,

I think my parents might get over the fact that she didn't become a doctor, or a lawyer, or whatever other professions were on their wish list."

"It's tough, isn't it," she mused, taking the mug of coffee Anthony handed her gratefully. "Trying to live your own life, with the constant expectations and pressures of your parents. And what would be good enough for one set doesn't seem to be for another."

"Mine were thrilled when I became a lawyer," Anthony agreed. "But for the last few years, it's like they don't see why I can't do that and be married with a brood of kids too."

"Do they point out other success stories? I get that all the time – 'Oh, but so and so is a doctor and is married, so it is possible.'"

Anthony laughed. "Worse, they are the success story! Both successful lawyers, married in their twenties and with four kids."

"Yeah, that is worse," Hannah agreed with a sigh. "At least I can excuse mine by saying they haven't got a clue how stressful medicine is."

Once they'd finished their coffees they took the bags upstairs, and found two double bedrooms made up in nautical themed bedding. Both had ensuites, and Hannah pulled out the silver dress before jumping in the shower. The drive down had been nothing but pleasant; there was no awkwardness between her and Anthony, even without alcohol, which was a relief.

But now she found she was nervous about wearing the dress. Alice the shop assistant had insisted it looked great, and Hannah had certainly felt good in it – but it was much more form-fitting than she normally wore. What if Anthony thought she looked stupid? Or her mother made some cutting remark as soon as they arrived at the party?

She may have had her reservations, but she also had nothing else suitable to wear, and so once she was out of the shower, and had blow-dried and straightened her mousy hair, she slipped the dress on, the fabric smooth against her skin. She'd bought a plunge bra, at Alice's suggestion, and when she looked in the mirror, she wasn't displeased...just nervous.

She put on the only jewellery she owned – a silver bangle and a locket necklace she'd received for her twenty-first birthday – and inexpertly applied some sparkly eyeshadow and eyeliner, hoping it didn't look too much like she'd let a child loose with a make-up pallet.

With a deep breath, she grabbed her handbag, slipped on the low silver heels, and headed downstairs.

They needed to leave fairly soon, and Anthony was already waiting downstairs, looking out to sea. She could see from behind that he had followed her advice on the black suit, but when he turned, she realised he'd paired it with a silver tie to adhere to the theme even more.

She met his eyes, and blushed as they widened.

"Wow, Hannah. You look incredible."

"Really?" she asked. "I wasn't sure about the dress..."

"Really," he said, his eyes following her as she descended the last couple of stairs and joined him by the window. "The dress looks great. Honestly."

She found herself wanting to disagree, to point out all the ways she was out of her comfort zone in it, but instead decided to simply accept the compliment.

"Thank you. You look great too – I love the tie."

"Well," he said, straightening the knot around his neck. "Thought it wouldn't hurt to embrace some silver, make your parents like me even more..."

Hannah rolled his eyes. "I don't think you need to try. Being there with me, and looking like that, and being a lawyer...it's plenty!"

Anthony laughed and gestured to the door. "Shall we?"

"Are you sure you don't mind driving? I feel bad you can't drink to get through this..."

"It's fine, honestly." He opened up the passenger door for her again, like he had done before. "Public transport seems pretty non-existent round here, let alone taxis. And since we need to leave at a reasonable time tomorrow, it'll be better if I have a clear head. You were a bad influence on me at my sister's wedding."

Anthony started the engine as Hannah protested. "I was the bad influence? I don't normally do shots. You were the one buying them!"

"And you were the one suggesting another round..."

CHAPTER ELEVEN

The ballroom of the hotel had been decorated with black and silver balloons, garlands, and candles, and with the sun still streaming through the windows, the place sparkled.

Anthony took her hand as they entered, and Hannah smiled. The feeling of his warm hand around hers was pleasant, and she knew it would help to convince her parents that they were an item. It also gave her a bit more confidence to walk in wearing the silver dress.

Mum and Dad were standing in the centre of the room, greeting their guests as they came in. Hannah held tightly onto Anthony's hand as they made their way across the dance floor and joined the group.

"Happy anniversary, Mum, Dad," Hannah said, when the guests in front left to get drinks.

"Hannah, darling. How lovely to see you. And that dress..."

"It's beautiful, isn't it?" Anthony jumped in, holding out his hand to shake Mum's. "Thank you so much for inviting me, Mrs Martin, Mr Martin. It's lovely to see you again."

Mum and Dad both shook his hand and beamed. "Thank you for coming! And your sister will be here soon too, she and Oscar said they were able to come."

"It looks like a great party," Hannah said, still holding Anthony's hand. She didn't know what comment her mum had been about to make about the dress, but she was very appreciative of Anthony jumping in with a compliment. He seemed so aware of what everyone around him was feeling. Perhaps that came from being a lawyer.

"Well, we're very glad you could come, both of you," Dad said with a genuine-looking smile. "And you look very smart in that dress, sweetheart."

Hannah smiled. "Thanks, Dad." More guests were waiting behind them to say hello to the hosts, so Hannah pulled at Anthony's hand. "We'll get a drink – we'll see you later."

When they got to the bar, where Hannah ordered herself a glass of wine and a Coke for Anthony, Anthony said, "See? That wasn't so bad, was it?"

"I suppose not," Hannah reluctantly agreed. "Although I think you probably cut Mum off before she could make some snarky comment about my dress."

"I'm sure she just doesn't realise how she comes across..."

Hannah nearly snorted. She was pretty sure her mother knew exactly how her words came across. "I'll remind you of how understanding you are when it's your parents we're dealing with, next month."

"Fair enough," Anthony said with a chuckle. "But that dress really does look great on you, so you mustn't take anything your mother says to heart."

Hannah's heart warmed at the sentiment. "Thanks, Anthony. I'm really glad we decided to do this."

He raised his glass of Coke to clink it against her wine glass. "So am I. Here's to the arrangement – long may it keep our parents off our backs."

"I'll drink to that."

"Hello, stranger," came a voice from behind them, and Hannah turned to find her cousin and his wife, Anthony's sister, Christi.

"Seeing you two months in a row, this must be some sort of record," Christi said, and Anthony let go of Hannah's hand to give Christi a hug.

"It's good to see you," Oscar said, reaching over to hug Hannah. He looked more bronzed than he had at the wedding, and Hannah tried to remember whether they had gone somewhere exotic for their honeymoon, or whether his tan was just from spending time outdoors over the sunny summer they'd had.

"Lovely to see you again too, Hannah," Christi said, leaning in for a hug. "Even if I can't understand why someone would voluntarily spend their free time with my big brother."

The four of them laughed, and Oscar and Christi ordered drinks at the bar, before they all headed out onto the terrace to enjoy the evening sunshine.

"So, are you staying at Alfie's parents' place?" Christi asked, sipping on a fruity cocktail.

Anthony nodded. "He offered, and I thought it made sense. It's only a few minutes from here. I would have gone to see him tomorrow, but we've both got to get back for work."

"No rest for the wicked, eh?" Oscar said.

"Something like that," Hannah said, watching the sun as it began to set over the ocean. It was nice to have a night off, but she certainly wasn't dreading work the following evening. Although perhaps, with Anthony not drinking, it made sense for her to limit her consumption so she didn't have a horrendous hangover to deal with on the drive home.

"You'll have to catch up next time you're down," Christi said. "And see his and Ivy's new place. They seem very happy, you know. I have to admit, I wasn't sure how it was going to work – the unexpected pregnancy, him living down here part-time. But it was his idea to move down here, from what Ivy tells me. And they seem to be thriving."

Anthony smiled. "I'm really pleased for them. I still can't quite believe that Alfie is a dad... But hey, I guess we all have to grow up sometime."

Oscar laughed. "We certainly do. One day marriage isn't even on your mind...and the next thing you know, you've got a wife and a bed-and-breakfast."

"Don't say that like it's a bad thing," Christi said, tapping his arm playfully.

"Oh, I promise you, it's only a good thing," Oscar said with an indulgent smile.

"Good. And don't think you can avoid scrutiny, Anthony. You know full well that I've always been the failure of the family–"

"Christi..." Anthony interjected.

"It doesn't bother me. But, you know, I think Mum and Dad think that my business is actually successful now and I'm actually married...so they'll be turning their critical eye on you and the rest."

Hannah laughed, and Anthony groaned. "I know you're right. But I'm not even the eldest! Surely they ought to be bothering Mark or Logan first."

Christi shrugged. "Well, it's not like they see Mark very often – although, did you hear? He's coming back from California for Dad's seventieth next month. Twice in one year, with my wedding – that really is a surprise! But I think Logan gets just as many hints about marriage as you do, don't worry." She flashed Hannah a smile. "Are you coming to Dad's birthday?"

"That's the plan," Hannah said.

"Excellent. Although I'm afraid Mum and Dad won't be subtle about what they're hoping..."

Hannah laughed again. "Don't worry – my parents haven't got a subtle bone in their bodies. I'm used to it."

The meal was served buffet-style, and Anthony and Hannah ended up sitting with Oscar and Christi again, as well as Aunt June, Oscar's mum. Mum and Dad looked exceptionally happy, and everyone applauded and took photos as an impressive three-tiered black and silver cake was brought out.

"Forty years," Anthony said with a wistful sigh. "Hard to imagine, isn't it?"

"It really is," Hannah agreed. "They married at twenty-two. I was still in uni at that age."

"Me too. My parents are the same – they celebrated their ruby anniversary a couple of years ago." He glanced over at Oscar and Christi beside them. "They could have forty years of marriage, maybe more."

Hannah had another glass of wine with her meal, but after that switched to orange juice, not wanting to end up drunk when Anthony was stone-cold sober. And she found, with him there, it wasn't as painful an experience as other family events had been.

He was extremely attentive. His hand hovered near her back when they walked together, or held her hand, and Hannah was fairly sure everyone believed they were a couple. She felt a little guilty lying to her parents, and to Christi and Oscar, but the easy atmosphere and lack of comments was surely worth it. And the following month, when they went to Edinburgh for Anthony's dad's birthday, she would hopefully make it just as easy for him.

It really was a win-win situation.

"How are you getting home?" Anthony asked Christi and Oscar, as they ordered more drinks at the bar.

"Aunt Olivia offered to pick us up," Christi said, glancing at the clock. "Although I did promise we wouldn't make it too late – she likes to go to bed pretty early!"

"Are you taking Aunt June home, too?" Hannah asked, glancing over at her aunt, who was sitting in an armchair and looking exhausted.

Oscar shook his head. "Your parents offered to book her a room here for the night, so she could come and join in, but go to bed whenever she was ready. She gets pretty tired these days... It was really thoughtful of them."

For a moment she saw her parents through his eyes. A whole evening of not having them comment on her being single, or when she was going to settle down, or when she would be having children, made it a lot easier to see the great people they really were.

She just wished they could stop obsessing over who she was going to spend her life with.

"Why don't I give you a lift home?" Anthony suggested. "I'm driving anyway, saves your aunt from having to come out to get you. And Hannah was saying on the way down that she wanted to see your B&B, so she could have a quick look?"

He glanced down at Hannah, as though to get her approval, and she smiled back at him. She'd mentioned in passing in the car that it was a shame she hadn't had time to see the B&B last time, and wouldn't this time either. She hadn't thought he would remember...

"Yeah, that sounds great, if you don't mind? I know you had a long drive down here this morning, you must be exhausted..."

"I think we're both used to long days and late nights," Anthony said.

"The perfect match!" Christi said with a glint in her eye.

Hannah glanced at Anthony, and wondered if he was also feeling slightly guilty about their deception. But in order to have both sets of parents believe in the match, it was of course necessary to have Christi and Oscar believe it too – as well as the rest of Anthony's brothers.

After a quick tour of the downstairs of the quaint B&B, with all the rooms rented out, Hannah and Anthony headed back to the holiday home. The roads were quiet, which was a blessing as poor Anthony had been forced to reverse so many times when they had driven to the hotel earlier that evening. She wasn't sure which was worse – driving in London, or driving on these tiny country lanes! She was certainly happy to only be a passenger.

"I enjoyed tonight," Anthony said when they got inside, loosening his tie and his top button. "Even sober."

"Me too," Hannah said. "And thank you – it was much easier with you here."

"Me pleasure." Their eyes met, and the contact was held for just a second too long. There was a frisson of...something in the air, but Hannah struggled to understand it. Was it just his good looks? Because neither of them was drunk, and there was no one here they needed to fool.

"Well... I guess we'd better get some sleep," she said,

breaking the moment.

"Early start tomorrow," Anthony agreed.

At the top of the stairs, they both paused, then said goodnight and disappeared into their separate rooms.

CHAPTER TWELVE

After the success of the ruby wedding anniversary party, Hannah was less nervous when the time came for Anthony to pick her up for the longer drive to Edinburgh for his dad's birthday party. She'd purchased yet another dress – she was getting quite a wardrobe now, after years of never taking the time off work to go to events like these – and although it was much simpler than the silver dress she had worn to the anniversary party, she was pleased with it. Alice had yet again come up with a winner – a little black number that Hannah planned to use to replace her staple little black dress whenever she needed to dress up.

Other than texting to arrange the time to meet, Hannah and Anthony hadn't communicated in the three weeks since the anniversary party. It was the benefit of the arrangement: between major family events, she didn't need to worry about losing herself in work and forgetting to stay in touch. And clearly Anthony felt the same, for although they'd had a good time – without any drunk kisses this time – he'd not been in touch either.

But that was fine by her. Once again he pulled up in his sports car outside her flat, took her bag and opened the door for her. And once again they stopped for coffee before setting off.

"So," she asked, as they made their way through the

morning traffic. "Anything I need to know before we get there? To make sure they don't catch on?"

"Not that I can think of... Both my brothers will be there – you met them at the wedding. Although that might have been after more than one shot..."

Hannah laughed. "Remind me again?"

"Logan is the doctor, he lives in Manchester. And then Mark lives in California, plays basketball for a living."

"Wow. Professionally?"

"Yep, left on a scholarship when he was eighteen and has never moved back."

She tried to picture him at the wedding, but the end of the evening was a bit of a blur. Surely he was fairly tall, if he played basketball? She remembered all three King brothers being good-looking, but not much besides that.

"And then you know Christi, of course. She's coming with Oscar."

"You see your family a lot," she commented, sipping her latte.

Anthony chuckled. "You know, I never really did? But lately, it does seem to be that way. I guess with Christi marrying, it's made everyone a bit more family minded."

"And more concerned with when their other three kids are getting married, I guess?" Hannah asked.

"You're right there. But I reckon Logan will take the brunt of the questions about his love life, since I'm bringing you." He smiled. "Sorry, though, if they make comments about marriage or kids..."

"Hey, that's what I'm here for. To deflect and move the focus onto another sibling. Imagine how it's been for me all these years – I don't even have a sibling to take the heat!"

The birthday party was a formal sit-down dinner

in a hotel on the Royal Mile in Edinburgh, followed by what Hannah was informed was a ceilidh. More than half the people there seemed to know the steps to the Scottish folk dances, but thankfully there was someone at the front to call out and demonstrate the steps, and Hannah wasn't the only clueless one.

By the end of their first dance together, Hannah was breathless and couldn't remember ever laughing so much.

"I thought I was fit!" she exclaimed, grabbing a drink from a passing waiter. "But that's more of a workout than any dance I've ever done before."

Anthony laughed. "They do it in PE lessons in school up here," he said.

"Did you go to school in Scotland?"

He shook his head. "No, Mum and Dad didn't move up here until I was heading off to uni. But I've been to a few ceilidhs with them, so I know some of the steps."

"You look like a natural," Hannah said. He somehow didn't even seem out of breath from the exuberant dance, and his eyes shone as he smiled.

"Are you coming to dance?" she asked Oscar and Christi, who were sat watching them from a nearby table.

"Not right now," Oscar said.

"But you two look good on the dance floor! Keep that up and Mum and Dad will be planning a ceilidh at your wedding before the night is through..."

Anthony rolled his eyes and Hannah laughed. It was nice to not feel any pressure from comments like those. And so far, she'd barely seen Anthony's parents. She and Anthony hadn't been seated very close to them on the long dining table, and now they were busy dancing and making the rounds of their guests. They'd greeted her warmly, though, and looked over approvingly as they danced – so she hoped the ruse was helping Anthony with his parents as much as it had helped Hannah with hers.

"Strip the Willow!" Anthony called, as the music started up again. Hannah frowned. "It's another dance. My favourite. Come on!"

He took her hand and pulled her onto the dance floor, and Hannah laughed and stumbled along behind him. She'd thought he'd be serious and sedate, being a lawyer, but he seemed keen to grab fun wherever he could.

And she was happy to go along for the ride.

Hannah got a break from dancing when Mark and Logan, Anthony's brothers, pulled them over to join them, Christi and Oscar for a drink. She and Logan chatted medicine for a while, until the others began to fake yawn, and the topic moved on to the weather in California.

"I have to keep a winter wardrobe here, for when I come over," Mark said. "No point packing all my thick jumpers and taking them back with me."

"How long are you here for?" Hannah asked.

"I've actually got a bit of a longer break, so I thought I'd stick around for a few weeks – make the most of the time over here. Otherwise it seems I just about get over the jet lag and then I'm heading back!"

"Are you sure you can cope with a Scottish winter, now you've gone all soft in California?" Logan asked, nudging him with his elbow.

Mark laughed. "I think I'll manage. It'll make a nice change, going for a run and not being hot the second I leave the door!"

"You know, you've been gone so long you're starting to get an American twang," Anthony said, and this was clearly a running joke, because they all started to put on terrible American accents.

Laughing, Hannah excused herself to find the bathrooms. The sound of someone vomiting hit her as soon as the door swung open, and she chose the furthest stall away, thinking that someone had clearly overdone it on the open bar.

But when she exited and turned the tap on, she was surprised to see Christi exiting the stall.

"You okay?" she asked, frowning at how pale she was. "Too much to drink?" But she couldn't remember seeing Christi with a single glass of wine.

"I'm fine," Christi said, splashing some cold water on her face.

"Are you sure? You look a bit pale..."

Christi nodded and turned to Hannah. "Please, don't say anything to anyone else."

Hannah frowned. "About what?"

She glanced to the toilet stall and then back at Hannah.

"That you're ill?"

Christi laughed. "I thought you were supposed to be a doctor?"

Hannah frowned for a minute, the alcohol making her own thoughts a little hazy, before putting two and two together.

"Oh! You're pregnant?"

Christi bit her bottom lip and nodded. "But it's early days, and we don't want to overshadow Dad's birthday. So just...keep it to yourself, okay?"

"I will," Hannah said, feeling dense for not thinking of the possibility earlier. After all, hadn't Anthony joked at their wedding that there would surely be Christenings in the near future? "Congratulations!" she said belatedly, and Christi grinned before ushering her back out into the crowded party.

CHAPTER THIRTEEN

The next event, shortly after Anthony's dad's birthday, was a party for Logan – thrown before Mark returned to California after a surprisingly long stay in the UK, so that the whole family could be together. It was in Manchester, and so once against they drove together, and checked into a fancy hotel where the party was being held.

"I'm sorry..." Anthony said as the hotel door swung open to reveal one king-size bed in the centre of the room. "When Mark said he was sorting rooms, I didn't even think about the sleeping arrangements. I'll go downstairs, see if they've got another room."

Hannah shook her head. She'd been surprised to see the king-size bed, but she supposed she shouldn't have been; as far as everyone else knew, she and Anthony had been dating for months. Of course they expected they would be sharing a bed.

"It's a tiny hotel," she said, putting her bag down on the dresser. "It's entirely booked up with people here for Logan's birthday."

"Well, maybe they have one with twin beds we can swap to, at least–"

"It's fine, Anthony. It's one night, it's a big bed, and we won't be back until late anyway."

"Are you sure? I don't want you to feel uncomfortable."

"It's fine," Hannah insisted, starting to feel a little irritated. She knew they were pretending, but would it kill him to share a bed with her for a night? Was she so repulsive to him that he couldn't stand the thought of being so close to her, even platonically?

They took it in turns showering and getting changed in the bathroom, before heading downstairs for the party. Logan had plenty of friends, as well as all his family, and the function room was already packed.

"Drink?" Anthony asked.

"Yeah, go on then – I'll have a small white wine."

He nodded and disappeared to the bar, while Hannah scanned the room for people she knew. She was getting more familiar with many people at these events: the King siblings, of course, as well as their parents, and a couple of aunts and uncles she now recognised. She hadn't socialised this much with people outside the hospital in years, but she found she didn't hate it. They expected her to be there, and were always happy to see her. She just wished she could shake her irritation at Anthony. It didn't even make sense. She didn't *want* to share a bed with him – she just wasn't stressed if she had to. And it was nice of him to not want her to feel awkward. So why did it feel so much like a rejection?

You need to go on some actual dates, she told herself. *Remind yourself that you are not on the shelf.* Better that than become needy with the guy she was in a pretend relationship with.

Christi and Oscar appeared in the crowd, and Hannah waved to them. They were the Kings – or, in truth the Reynolds – she knew the best, and she always liked catching up with her cousin. It was an unforeseen bonus of the arrangement with Anthony, this time where she got to get to know her cousin again as an adult.

"Hey," she called, embracing Oscar then Christi. "Oh wow, Christi, you're starting to show!"

Christi beamed and ran a hand over her slightly rounded stomach. "I know, I think I actually look somewhat pregnant now, and not like I've just been overeating."

"Definitely pregnant. How far gone are you now?"

"Fourteen weeks," Christi answered.

"And how's it going?" Hannah noticed Anthony looking around for her and waved him over.

"Well, I don't want to put you off," Christi said with a grimace. "But I am not a fan of pregnancy. The vomiting, the exhaustion..."

"Hopefully that will wear off soon," Hannah said sympathetically. "Although you don't need to worry about putting me off. I've never thought the whole experience was very appealing!"

"The baby at the end of it will be worth it though," Christi said, smiling at Oscar. "Just got to make it to that point!"

Anthony greeted them both and handed Hannah her glass of wine. "Did Aunt Olivia come with you two?" he asked.

"Yeah, she's over chatting to Logan now."

"It's nice that she comes to these family events, now that you're living down there."

Christi frowned. "I'm not sure how welcome she felt before, to be honest."

"Well, you know what Mum and Dad are like," Anthony said with a roll of his eyes. "Don't like anything that goes against the grain."

"Tell me about it."

"But they've already mentioned to me more than once how thrilled they are to be becoming grandparents, so I don't think you are playing the role of wayward daughter any more!"

Christi laughed. "They still think my choice of career is a bit left field...but you're right, the being married and having a baby thing has certainly improved me in their estimations. They wanted to be grandparents – they were just waiting for one of us to get on with it. You can't complain, though," she said, glancing at Hannah. "Now you've been with Hannah a few months, it's Mark and Logan who are getting the regular phone calls about the direction of their lives."

Anthony caught Hannah's eye and they both grinned. She was surprised to find how much that secret moment between them lifted her mood.

"It has been nice to avoid the weekly calls that oh-so-subtly tried to find out what was happening in my love life, I must say," Anthony said.

"Whereas with me it was about my career," Christi countered. "But they seem to have accepted me running the B&B and doing the ad work for the campsite, even if they're not thrilled about it."

They were interrupted by a slew of relatives wanting to congratulate Christi, and Hannah and Anthony slipped back, letting them have their moment in the limelight.

"Shall we go and say happy birthday to Logan?" Hannah suggested, nodding over in the direction of Anthony's brother, who seemed to have had a lull in people crowding around him.

Logan had clearly had a few drinks, and enthusiastically pulled them both into a hug. "Thank you both for coming!" he cried out, right next to Hannah's ear.

She looked at Anthony and laughed. "You're very welcome. Happy birthday! Are you enjoying the party?"

He nodded. "I don't normally like big gatherings, but this is fun! All my friends, and my family... Oh, Hannah, a load of friends from work are over in the corner. You should say hi – they always like to meet fellow doctors!"

"I'll do that," Hannah said, privately thinking she'd need to have drunk a lot more to go over and introduce herself to a group of unknown doctors. She was sure they would have a lot in common – after all, no one else seemed to quite understand the pressures and the thrill of the job – but she was actually quite happy just hanging out with Anthony, and Christi and Oscar. It was a routine she quite enjoyed at these family events. She talked about medicine enough every day, and with the friends she hung out with after work. She didn't *have* to discuss it at parties, too.

She loved her job. But it was nice to have a life outside of it.

The eldest King, Mark, stood up and called for the attention of the crowd. Everyone turned to him expectantly. He was tall, muscled, and his brown hair was lighter than that of both his brothers, possibly because the Californian sun had bleached it after so many years of living out there.

"I would just like us to raise a toast to my brother Logan. I don't get to come to many family functions, and it's wonderful to celebrate my little brother turning thirty. Thank you all for coming, and a very happy birthday to Logan!" He raised his pint, and everyone raised whatever they were drinking and repeated the words.

The rest of the evening passed in a blur of drinking, eating, and dancing. Anthony seemed to be good at dancing no matter what the music, and Hannah found she enjoyed the feeling of his hands on her waist as they swayed to some slow song.

She *really* needed to get out more if that little contact from a good-looking man sent her blood racing.

Towards the end of the evening, Anthony's parents sought them out as they were finishing off their drinks before heading back to the dance floor.

"Hannah, it's wonderful to see you again," Mr King said with a warm smile. Anthony's parents seemed to genuinely like her, which she hadn't really expected. She wondered how they'd feel if they knew she was just friends with their son. "We know how hard it is for doctors to get time off!"

Hannah smiled. "As long as I get enough advance warning, I can usually swing it."

"Family is important," Mrs King said. "It's so nice that Mark was still here, too. It's so rare to have all four of my children in the same room..."

"You almost sound sentimental, Mum," Anthony said with a chuckle. "That's not like you!"

"It must be the wine," she said with a small smile. "But it's good to see you two together, and so happy. It's a shame we only see you at big events though, Hannah – we never get to speak properly!"

"That is a shame," Hannah agreed. She only saw, or spoke to, Anthony at big events – so she was hardly going to start having cosy lunch dates with his parents. That would be weird – like they were actually dating. And besides, they lived all the way in Edinburgh.

"You can bring Hannah to visit, you know, Tony!" Mrs King said, with a disapproving look towards her son.

"You know how busy we are, Mum," Anthony said. "It's not that easy..."

"Hmm. Well, perhaps we'll come and see you sometime. There's plenty of space in that new place of yours, isn't there?"

Hannah raised an eyebrow. "New place?" She didn't remember him mentioning moving.

Mr King frowned. "Surely you've seen Tony's new house?"

Hannah swore in her head. The problem with not speaking in between family events was that they only caught up on a few superficial details while they were driving to wherever they needed to be. They didn't really *know* each other. It was all fake.

"Yeah, of course I have. Sorry, I thought you meant he was moving offices," she bluffed, hoping they wouldn't notice the slip-up.

Mrs King frowned. "Are you, Tony? You didn't mention that."

Anthony shook his head. "No, it was just an idea that was floated. But we like where we are. And yes, the new place has plenty of space. Hannah loves the garden, don't you?" he said, tossing her a lifeline.

"Oh yeah, it's great," she said, not saying anything specific in case it came back to bite her.

"But you and Dad are so busy with work, too," Anthony continued. "Don't stress yourselves out about coming down."

"We'd like to see you both," Mr King said. "In a less busy setting."

Anthony looked at Hannah. This would test the

arrangement, that was certain. Anthony had never been inside her home, and she had never even been to Oxford, where he lived.

"I'm sure we can figure something out," Hannah said with a smile. "It's just a question of figuring out our schedules."

When his parents disappeared, and Anthony and Hannah headed back to the dance floor, Anthony was apologetic.

"They never come and visit me," he said with a sigh. "They expect us to go to them, because they've got the bigger house and the busy work schedules..."

"Because you obviously just sit around and don't work," Hannah said with a roll of her eyes. "They obviously want to see us together."

"Yeah, I don't know if they're suspicious? Or maybe just want to lay some heavier hints about marriage with only the two of us there. We don't have to do it. We can make it so our rotas never line up."

"I don't mind," Hannah said. "If it fits in all right with work."

He tipped his head and smiled. "Thanks."

"But you need to keep me better informed. I nearly blew everything with that comment about your new place."

"I didn't even think about it. I'll make sure you know of any major changes in my life next time!"

"Good. Your parents are lawyers – they'll sniff out the truth if we're not careful, and then they'll hate me and be angry with you."

"I don't think they'd hate you," he said with a shrug. "They seem pretty invested in us."

"Do you feel bad?" she asked, biting her bottom lip.

"That they're all expecting we're heading down the aisle, and we're just going to end up disappointing them?"

He paused for a moment. It was a good job the song was slow, so his momentary freeze wasn't too noticeable. "No, we shouldn't feel guilty," he said eventually. "We never said anything about marriage. That's all them. We're just keeping them happy...until there is someone in our lives they *can* get excited about."

But when will that be? Hannah asked herself as they took the lift up to their hotel room at the end of the night. *Never, if you never go out and meet anyone, Hannah Martin.*

CHAPTER FOURTEEN

A little tipsy, they stumbled into their hotel room. Hannah had pretty much forgotten that there was only one bed, and her earlier irritation at Anthony's seeming reluctance to share it with her.

"Would you like the bathroom first?" Anthony asked, gesturing towards it.

"Thanks." Hannah grabbed her pyjamas, which were thankfully not too ancient –something she hadn't thought about, considering she hadn't expected to be sharing a room – and disappeared into the bathroom. She slipped off the black and gold jumpsuit she had worn for the occasion and started taking her make-up off. Her mother had always instilled in her how important it was to remove her make-up before bed, so no matter how drunk or exhausted she was, she always tried to remember.

She had only been in there a few minutes when there was a knock at the door. "Sorry, Hannah. Can I just grab my glasses?" Hannah frowned. She couldn't remember ever seeing him in glasses.

Making sure her pyjama top was fully buttoned, she opened the door to find a smiling Anthony on the other side.

"Sorry. I took my lenses out, and then realised I'd left my glasses in my wash bag in here. Logan is texting some drunken nonsense, and I can't really see to reply."

She slid to one side to allow him to enter, and as he moved past her into the small bathroom, his body brushed against hers. It was surely the alcohol that made such minor contact send delicious tingles through her body.

"See, that's another thing I didn't know – that you wore lenses, that you needed glasses. We're not very good at this whole faking a relationship thing."

Anthony laughed. "Sorry. I wear lenses all the time, just take them out to sleep. And since we've not slept together..."

Hannah found herself blushing, even though it was simply a statement of fact.

"And besides, when I hold your hand and dance with you, it seems to be enough to persuade everyone that we're together."

"That's true. I certainly haven't had any suspicious questions from my parents. Anyway, do you want to get in here? I'm done."

She climbed into bed and tried to remember the last time she had shared a bed with someone. She wasn't particularly one for one-night-stands, and on the rare occasions she did go home with someone, she never spent the whole night. Ironically, sharing a bed with her fake boyfriend was probably the most intimate she had been with a man since...well, since she could remember.

Anthony exited the bathroom with his dark-framed glasses on, looking rather adorably nerdy.

"You look more like a lawyer with the glasses," Hannah commented.

"Oh yeah?" Anthony raised an eyebrow. "Otherwise it's not believable?"

Hannah laughed. "It's not not believable. You're just a bit too good-looking to be a lawyer." Her cheeks flushed red as soon as she said it. She blamed the alcohol for letting such a thought escape her head unfiltered. Not that there was any falsehood in what she was saying; he was very good-looking. That was surely universally acknowledged. And that didn't fit with the picture she had in her head of what a lawyer looked like.

Still, there wasn't really any need to tell him she thought he was attractive.

But he just laughed, his eyes crinkling. "What about you? Every time I see you, you're dressed up in another gorgeous outfit. It's hard to picture you in scrubs pulling an all-night shift in A&E."

Hannah felt her cheeks redden even more. "Believe me, when you see me, it's the exception to the standard."

He slipped into bed beside her, and she could feel the warmth of his body even though they left a gap between them. He propped himself up on one elbow and turned to face her. "I know these events have been more about my family so far. But I really appreciate you doing it – it's made my life a lot simpler."

"Mine too," Hannah said with a soft smile. "And I have to admit… I've had fun."

"So have I…"

Something changed then. The air in the room became charged, and Hannah felt as though she couldn't properly breathe. He was looking at her with those deep brown eyes, and her heart was racing, her skin suddenly warm. The alcohol buzzed pleasantly through her veins, and she didn't know who moved first, but the next thing she knew, their lips were meeting in the middle of that king-size bed.

This felt very different from a drunken kiss on a dance floor in the dark, when they had to pretend to the world that they were a couple.

This was private, unexpected, and it felt surprisingly right...

The gap between them closed, and Hannah ran a hand through his soft, dark hair, pulling him closer as the kiss deepened. She hadn't expected this...but she certainly didn't want to push him away.

It would complicate everything, but she couldn't bring herself to care.

Not right now.

She had no idea what would have happened if that knock on the door hadn't come just as his hands slipped around her waist. At first they both ignored it, or didn't hear it, but then it came again, louder and more insistent, and Anthony pulled away. His eyes were wide, his pupils dilated, and Hannah had no idea what to say.

Then there was another knock. "Anthony? Are you in there?"

It was Mrs King's voice. Anthony jumped out of bed, and checked his appearance was decent before heading to the door. Hannah pulled the duvet over her, part of her embarrassed at being caught – although they had only been kissing, and the family did think they were together – and part of her frustrated by the interruption.

Right now, she really wanted to know where that kiss was going to lead.

Anthony opened the door a fraction, and sure enough Mrs King was standing on the other side. "Sorry to knock so late, dear. But your brother is drunk downstairs and doesn't want to go to bed, and Mark can't get him up on his own."

Anthony rolled his eyes. "That will damage his reputation of being the strong, sporty one of us all."

"I know you were going to bed, but could you come down and give us a hand?" She looked past Anthony to Hannah, who was still in bed, trying to process everything that had happened. "Hello, Hannah dear. Sorry for the intrusion..."

"No problem," she squeaked out. She didn't know why she was embarrassed. She was a grown woman, after all. And as far as Mrs King knew, she and Anthony had been dating for months.

She didn't know there was potentially something more going on in that room.

"Just give me a second to put a jumper on," Anthony said, pushing the door to and grabbing a jumper from his suitcase.

"Sorry about this..." he muttered.

"Don't worry," Hannah said, because what else could she say?

With his jumper over his pyjamas, he disappeared from the room, and Hannah leant back against the pillows with a sigh.

Her lips still tingled from that kiss. And she had wanted it to continue. She definitely had been happy to see where things went...

But now that he was gone, and the tension in the room had dissipated, common sense came flooding back.

What was she doing?

This was a fake relationship – and it had been working well. No need to stay in contact during the busy weeks at work, no guilt for not making enough time. Just a fun date to family events, with the bonus of having their parents off their backs.

What were they doing, complicating things?

Did she even like him like that?

She thought about it for a moment, listening out to the sounds of the hotel guests going to bed – doors banging, footsteps in the hallway, someone drunkenly singing. Was she attracted to him?

Yes, she supposed she was. But he was devastatingly handsome – she couldn't imagine what woman wouldn't be.

His brothers were good-looking, too – but, as the hotel door reopened, she had to admit that she didn't feel the same attraction to them as she did to Anthony.

But that didn't have to mean anything...

"Sorry about that," Anthony said, pulling his jumper over his head. As he did so, he accidentally lifted his pyjama top, flashing some seriously toned abs, which didn't help Hannah's resolve to be sensible. She didn't want to throw away an arrangement that was working perfectly well for a drunken night of passion.

"No worries. Is Logan okay?"

Anthony laughed. "He'll have a hangover tomorrow, but he's fine. He wanted the party to carry on all night – he's definitely overdone it, celebrating turning thirty. It'll give us something to tease him about for the next ten years."

Hannah laughed too but couldn't help noticing that Anthony was hovering awkwardly by the bed. It certainly seemed more of an issue, sharing a bed, after that kiss.

"We should probably get some sleep," Hannah said hurriedly, unable to handle the anticipation, unsure of what the right decision was. "We've got an early start tomorrow, and I've definitely had one too many glasses of wine..."

She knew she was giving herself an excuse, an excuse for the kiss, for her part in it. It was better, she told herself, if it was all just forgotten now – a drunken kiss between friends that, thankfully, hadn't gone any further.

"Oh," Anthony said, and she thought she detected a hint of surprise in his voice. "Yeah, sure. You're working tomorrow night, aren't you?"

Hannah nodded. "Probably shouldn't have drunk so much. But at least I'm not in as bad a state as Logan."

"Definitely not," Anthony said, flicking the light switch off and plunging them into darkness before climbing into bed himself. The bed sagged a little under his weight, and she felt the warmth from his body even with the gap between them. She resisted the urge to shuffle closer.

Don't lose your mind, Hannah, she told herself.

"Goodnight, then," Anthony said, and she heard the click of his glasses as he placed them on the bedside table.

"Goodnight," she said, even though she knew it would be a long time before she would manage to fall asleep. She couldn't, for the life of her, figure out if she was making the right decision – or a terrible one.

CHAPTER FIFTEEN

"So, you slept with him?" Jasmine asked, over a dinner of burgers and chips in the pub opposite the hospital. It was only three in the afternoon, so not really the hour for dinner, but the three of them had been working since the early hours of the morning.

"No," Hannah said, adding copious amounts of vinegar to her chips. "Well, I slept next to him, eventually...but nothing happened."

Eloise frowned. "But you kissed?"

"Yeah..."

"And he's hot?"

"Yeah..." Hannah conceded.

"Then why did nothing happen?" Jas asked.

Hannah sighed. She'd hoped to get some perspective from her friends, but they seemed to just think she was crazy for not sleeping with the hot lawyer she'd been pretending to date for months.

And maybe she was.

The drive home had been more awkward than usual, and she hadn't heard from him since he'd dropped her off – not that she normally did, after family events.

Why should anything be different now?

*Because of that kiss...*a voice in the back of her head said. But that wasn't fair. The kiss had been interrupted, and she'd made no moves to reignite the flame.

And she'd pre-empted any attempt he might have made by saying she had to sleep.

"I don't know..." she said with a groan. "I guess...this arrangement has been working well. It's uncomplicated, we have a good time, our parents are happy and not harassing us... Drunkenly hooking up seemed like it would ruin all of that."

"Or make it all much better," Eloise said with a smirk.

"Yeah, what if it became real?" Jasmine, ever the romantic, said. "What an amazing story that would be!"

"It was a drunken kiss," Hannah insisted. "Nothing more than that."

"How do you know that, unless it happens again?" Jasmine asked.

"Have you got a photo of him?" Eloise chimed in.

"Uh..." She scrolled through her phone, trying to remember if they'd ever had a photo taken together. "Oh, there's one at the wedding, I'm sure, let me just..."

The photographer had been taking photos of couples, groups, and families during the evening, and had snapped one of Hannah and Anthony, which Christi had then sent to Hannah. It was a photo of herself that she actually liked; the green dress made her look like she actually had curves, and Anthony was standing by her side, his arm slung around her waist, a broad smile on his handsome face.

She showed them both the photo, and was unsurprised by their responses. Anthony did look pretty great.

"And you've only kissed him twice? In all these months? You need your head testing!" Eloise said.

"You two look great together. And that dress, Han?

I've never seen you like that!"

Hannah blushed. "Well, there's not much call for fancy dresses in A&E, is there. Or our nights here, in the pub."

"Well, you look good. And he is gorgeous. I think you should mention the kiss, see what he says..."

Hannah wrinkled her face. "That's just going to be awkward."

"And is it not going to be awkward next time you have some family event, and you're pretending to be a couple, knowing that you actually kissed for real?"

Hannah groaned. "Yes. I guess."

"Well then."

Even though she could see the logic, Hannah did not contact Anthony, and she did not think she could face bringing up the kiss in person. That was if they saw each other any time soon: there were no other family functions in the calendar. Perhaps, after the kiss, he just wouldn't get in touch again.

And could she bring herself to ask him to accompany her to an event? With how confused that kiss made her?

She wasn't sure she could, even though she knew she was being pathetic about it.

So she did what she always did, and threw herself into work. It wasn't difficult; there were always extra shifts to be taken, and she'd had more weekends off in recent months than she had in years. But then Christmas came on the horizon, and the inevitable question from her parents about what her plans were.

She'd worked several of the previous Christmases, but she happened not to be rota-ed for this one. She was sure she could find someone desperate to swap, if she wanted the excuse... But she did always feel bad about working. After all, she *was* an only child, and it didn't seem totally fair on her parents, however much they wound her up sometimes.

But then they'd surely want to know why she wasn't spending it with Anthony... And it would be hard to fob them off.

By mid-December, when everyone had their trees up and Christmas carols filled every radio station, she still hadn't made a decision, and hadn't heard from Anthony in weeks. And so, after a couple of post-work glasses of wine, she decided she ought to message him.

Are you getting grilled over your Christmas plans too?

She was alone in the pub; everyone else was still working, or off that night. The place was packed with people enjoying the Christmas spirit, but she sat alone in the back corner, feeling rather bah humbug about it all.

She'd never been a huge fan of Christmas. It always seemed like so much effort for one day. The magic had been lost the day she'd found out the truth about Father Christmas, and it had never returned.

It was a day where people inevitably drank too much, sustained burns, fought with their families, and tripped over piles of presents – so a busy day for the accident and emergency department.

When her phone buzzed only minutes later, she found herself grinning.

Yes – endlessly. They want me at Christmas, want us at Christmas, want us to be spending it together... I don't think I can win whatever I do!

She was still smiling as she replied: *I might work it. I'll get disappointed faces, but no expectations!*

He replied almost instantly. *I don't think I can say*

I need to work, people aren't usually desperate for lawyers on Christmas day… Mark's not home, Christi and Oscar are spending it with her aunt, and Logan is working (you doctors have it so easy.) So it'll just be me and my parents!

Hannah laughed. *Try being an only child – it's always only me and the parents!*

The texts continued back and forth over the evening, and she was so engaged with them that she didn't even notice how long she had sat on her own until Jasmine sat down opposite her.

"I can't believe you're still here! I was stuck in that surgery for hours. I thought you'd have gone home."

Hannah glanced up at her, a little dazed from staring at her phone for so long. Had it really been hours?

"Why are you looking so…starry-eyed?"

Hannah blushed and blinked her eyes. "I'm not. Just tired."

Jasmine didn't look convinced. "Why are you clutching your phone?"

"I'm not clutching it. Look, shall we eat? I'm starving," she said, changing the subject.

Anthony was just as easy to talk to over text as in person – and she was pleased to find the kiss hadn't changed anything between them.

They hadn't messaged before, except to arrange meeting places. Would she always have been so pleased to hear from him? She couldn't remember – and before Jasmine could accuse her of being 'starry-eyed' again, she pulled the menu towards her and ignored her phone buzzing on the table.

Three days later, still undecided, she got a surprising phone call just after lunch.

"I'm not disturbing you at work, am I?"

The sound of his voice made her smile, though she couldn't understand why.

"No, Anthony, I'm not working till tonight. Is everything okay?" She wanted to point out that he didn't usually ring, and ask if there was a reason he was doing so out of the blue, but she presumed he would get to the point.

"Good. I just wanted to catch you quickly..."

Her heart began to race. Was he going to bring up the kiss? Was this the awkward moment she had been dreading?

"She hasn't got round to sending invitations yet, but Christi's friend Ivy – her maid of honour, if you remember?"

Hannah nodded, then realised of course he couldn't see her.

"Yeah, I remember her."

"Well, she's organising a baby shower for both Christi and Oscar – apparently sometimes these things are done as a couples' thing. I can't say I've ever been to one, so I don't really know much about it."

Hannah laughed. "I don't think I have either." It didn't seem like he was going to mention the kiss, for which she was rather grateful.

"Well, it's going to be in January, and I thought we could go together... If you're still up for the arrangement, that is." He sounded slightly awkward, and she thought that was probably the closest they were going to get to mentioning what had happened.

"Yeah, I'm up for it," she said without pausing to think. Clearly, they could have a conversation without it being ridiculously awkward. And if he didn't want to mention it, then she wouldn't either. They could go on as if it hadn't happened. Just a silly drunken kiss that no one ever needed to know about. "It's in Devon, I presume?"

"Yeah, on the fifteenth, I think. I'm not sure why it's so early, but I didn't really ask questions. Christi insisted she'd want both of us there, so I thought I'd better check in with you before I gave any responses."

"It's nice of Christi to invite me. And it definitely sounds like a situation for the arrangement. Nothing gets parents more interested in when they'll have grandchildren than the baby shower of a relative."

"My thinking exactly," Anthony said. "I don't want to face that without you by my side."

Hannah felt butterflies in her stomach at his words, which she knew wasn't sensible. He didn't mean anything by it. She didn't want him to mean anything by it. He was just a good-looking guy who she happened to have kissed...

"So, did you make a decision about Christmas?" he asked, and they spent nearly an hour chatting about their lives and what was going on – so that they weren't caught out with a lack of knowledge, of course.

For the first time ever, Hannah arrived at work five minutes late, having not noticed the time slipping away while she sat talking to Anthony.

They decided, together, that they would spend Christmas with their parents individually – and if grilled about why they weren't spending it together, they could each say how important their own family was to them, earning more brownie points. Then, come January, they could back this story up with each set of parents. It was perfect, really. Her parents would be thrilled that she was in a relationship, and thrilled that she was spending

Christmas with them.
Everyone won.
She just had to remember that it wasn't real...

CHAPTER SIXTEEN

The texts between them, and the odd phone call, continued throughout December, and on Christmas morning, Hannah fired off a quick text: *Quick, my parents want to know what I got you for Christmas. Any ideas?*

I wouldn't want to spoil my surprise, came the immediate response, accompanied by a winking emoji.

I can't stall much longer, and my brain is blank! she replied quickly.

"Hannah, are you even listening to me?" her mum asked, and Hannah looked up from her phone with a guilty smile. She definitely hadn't been.

"Sorry, Mum," she said, unable to wipe the smile off her face. "I was just texting Anthony."

It was nice to have someone to blame for her distraction, but she hadn't anticipated the number of questions that admitting she was texting him would encourage.

"Is he having a nice time with his parents?" her mum asked, picking up a stray piece of wrapping paper that had ended up stuck in the carpet.

"I think so," Hannah responded, though she hadn't actually asked him much about his Christmas Day. "It's just him and his parents this year, so quite a quiet one. For him, at least." For Hannah and her parents, every year was just the three of them – except the years when Hannah worked, and then it was just Mum and Dad. She wondered what it must have been like to grow up in such a big family, with three siblings. How hectic those Christmas mornings must have been.

"You two have been going out, what, five months now?" her mum asked.

Hannah counted the months from the wedding and nodded. "Yeah, something like that."

"It's the longest you've been with anybody in a long time. Things are getting serious."

Hannah squirmed under her mother's intense gaze. This was the problem with the arrangement – when she had to outright lie. But at least it saved her from being told how disappointing it was that she didn't have anyone in her life.

"We're just having fun, Mum. Not stressing about whether it's serious or not." She didn't want to give her mum too much hope. After all, at some point, the arrangement would come to an end – although hopefully, she'd have someone else for her parents to meet by then, to soften the blow.

"Well, he seems like a lovely young man," her dad said, sipping the fancy beer Hannah had bought him for Christmas. "It'll be nice to see him at the baby shower. And perhaps you could bring him to stay sometime, so we can get to know him a bit better."

It was not dissimilar to Anthony's parents' insistence on seeing them outside of family events, so she supposed she shouldn't be surprised. "Oh, yeah... Well, we'll have to see what we can do with our schedules... He's very busy, you know, and I..."

Mum tutted. "Honestly, Hannah. You've got a boyfriend now, you can't always both be too busy to see anybody. You won't see each other at this rate!"

Hannah forced a smile. No matter what she did, there was always criticism. And Mum was rather close to the truth; they never *did* see each other outside family events. That was why this worked so well.

She rang him that night. She wasn't sure why; there was nothing that needed to be discussed. But there was something about being back in her childhood bedroom (because she'd decided if she was going to spend Christmas with her parents, she couldn't be doing with trying to get back into the city late at night) that made her feel like her life wasn't really moving forwards. She loved her job, but it was slow progress to the consultant position she wanted. And other than in work, had anything in her life changed in the last five years?

She was still in the same flat, even though she could afford someplace bigger. She hadn't had a serious relationship in that time, either. Now there was Anthony – but he wasn't real.

So why was she ringing him? She couldn't really say, except that it felt right, in the moment.

He answered after two rings.

"Did you figure out what you bought me for Christmas?" he asked in that deep, sexy voice of his.

She laughed. "No thanks to you. A book of Shakespeare quotes for every day of the year."

Anthony chuckled. "Because I'm such a great fan of the Bard?"

"Because it was all I could think of. I'd seen it in a shop last week. Do you like Shakespeare?"

"Not really, I'm afraid. I was always far more into science than literature..."

"Me too. Well, when my parents ask, make sure you

know something about Shakespeare, okay?"

"Did you make me out to be some kind of aficionado?" he asked.

"Well, I'm not sure. They had a lot of questions tonight, about you, and I've lied a lot. So just don't drop me in it."

She sat down on her single bed as she heard him sigh. "Yeah, I've had the questions too. All the heat on me, with the others not here."

"Has it been a good Christmas?" she asked, crossing her legs.

"It's been fine. I'm not that into the whole festive season, you know?"

Hannah laughed. "Me, neither. But most people think you're a terrible person if you don't love it!"

"Edinburgh is pretty at this time of year. The lights are pretty amazing, and there's a huge Christmas market."

"A few of my friends have always said about going, but we've never got round to it," Hannah said, thinking back over the many years of aborted plans because one of them was working.

"But it's a lot when it's just me, and my parents are so interested in my life! Last year it was why wasn't I dating anyone, when would I settle down, didn't I know there was more to life than work..."

Hannah snickered. "Oh yes, I've had many years like that."

"But this year it was where is Hannah, aren't you spending it with her, are things serious, do you love her..."

"Wow, they're more direct than my parents," Hannah said, irritated that her cheeks had flushed pink at this man mentioning the word love. What a ridiculous reaction.

"Oh yes, they don't hold back. Seems we just swapped one set of questions for another, eh?"

"I guess. But it's quite nice not being such a disappointment any more..."

She heard muffled noises on the end of the line. "Sorry, Hannah, I've got to go and deal with a Christmas tree emergency."

Hannah couldn't help but laugh. "Everyone okay?"

"Yes, just the cat stuck up it I think. Merry Christmas, and I'll see you soon."

"Merry Christmas, Anthony."

As she lay in her single bed that night, struggling to fall asleep, she wondered what it would be like to have a *real* boyfriend. The question sounded ridiculously juvenile in her mind, and she knew in the past, relationships hadn't worked out. Men expected her to be there, to put them first, to be able to meet at a moment's notice. To never cancel, or forget important dates, because her work was just so hectic.

But there were nice parts to being in a relationship, too. Phone calls before bed. Someone to get dressed up with and go out. Curling up on the sofa and watching a film. Having someone care about how your day was...

Pretending made everything easier. But perhaps, with the right person, a real relationship wouldn't be impossible.

It had been two months since she'd seen him, and when she waited on the pavement for him in the middle of January, her big coat wrapped tightly around her and a present in one hand, she felt both nervous and excited.

It was silly to feel either, really. They'd spoken

plenty in the interim, and they'd done this several times before, so she knew what to expect.

Except...they hadn't been away together since The Kiss. The Kiss that was never mentioned again.

They'd been offered Alfie's parents' holiday home again, since they didn't use it much in the winter, and so she at least knew that they would definitely have the option of separate bedrooms. It would be easy to pretend nothing had happened, and carry on with things as before.

And then, now that they'd begun a new year, she'd resolved to start going out on more dates. The arrangement wasn't a permanent thing, and if she wanted to find someone real, and not have her parents be devastated whenever she and Anthony decided to dissolve this partnership, she needed to get out there.

It was a shame that even thinking of first dates made her cringe.

He pulled up in his red sports car, and when he got out he flashed her a heart-stopping smile. She really had forgotten how handsome he was in the two months since she'd seen him.

"Hello, stranger," he said, taking the present from her and opening the door. "I got a present too...should we have gone in on it together? Will they think it's weird?"

"Hmm," Hannah said as she got into the blissful warmth of the car. "Maybe. We could put them in the same bag, say they're from both of us? Unless you got something really tacky..."

Anthony laughed as he fastened his seatbelt and started the engine, heading towards their usual coffee stop before the journey down to Devon. "I got a baby blanket that I know my sister will love."

"That sounds okay," Hannah said with a smile. "I got a baby memory book, so they should go well together. And then the cards–"

"I didn't think to get a card," Anthony said sheepishly.

Hannah rolled her eyes. "I'll see if we can open mine, scrawl your name, and reseal it without it looking a mess."

CHAPTER SEVENTEEN

They arrived at the B&B, where Ivy was hosting the baby shower, at the same time as Anthony's brother, Logan.

Anthony shifted the gift bag – which now held both presents and a hastily amended card – to his other hand, so he could take Hannah's as they walked up to the door.

They'd held hands many times as part of this ruse, but now his hand felt warmer around hers, stronger, more comforting. She didn't have time to analyse her feelings, though, as Logan pulled them both into a bear hug. She thought he was the most exuberant of the King siblings, with a friendly smile and a twinkle in his eye that made you feel at ease.

"Great to see you both," he said, releasing them. "Sorry I missed you at Christmas, Anthony."

"Well, you should be sorry for leaving me to deal with Mum and Dad on my own. But I suppose I have to forgive you," Anthony said with a smirk.

"You know how it is, I can't control the rota," Logan replied, flashing Hannah a smile. "Isn't that right, Hannah?"

Hannah nodded. "I've worked plenty of Christmases and New Years, and every other occasion you can think of. It's just how the job is."

"Exactly." Logan gave his brother a smug smile. "Makes a love life pretty impossible, though, when you're never sure when you'll be working or for how long, or whether you'll even make it home when you said you would. Something Mum and Dad don't seem to understand..."

He ran a hand through his hair. "But, I mean, it can work. You two are proof of that. Two high-powered jobs, and you still seem happy – what's the secret?"

Hannah squeezed Anthony's hand a little tighter. The secret, of course, was no expectations and no commitments. But she couldn't tell Logan that.

It was something she needed to remind herself of. This felt so perfect, so dreamlike, because it wasn't real. She never had to cancel plans at the last minute, never had to explain why she wouldn't be home for dinner or couldn't make a date. She hadn't left him alone while she worked night after night, not even knowing if it was day or night by the end of it.

The front door opened, sparing Hannah from having to come up with a lie. Ivy stood on the other side, her long brown hair flowing down her back, a big smile on her face.

"I thought I heard voices. Come in, come in, it's freezing out here. Oscar and Christi are in the dining room..."

They followed Ivy in, nearly tripping over her crawling daughter, Rose, as they did. "Out of the way, darling, you can't crawl here right now," Ivy said, sweeping up the little girl and carrying her on her hip.

Christi sat in a comfortable chair in the living room, looking far more pregnant than the last time Hannah had seen her. Oscar was chatting beside her to

Christi's aunt Olivia, but aside from that, they were the first guests to arrive.

Christi beamed at them. "You made it in good time," she said, placing her hands on the armrests to push herself up.

"Don't get up," Hannah said, hurrying over to give her a hug. "We'll come to you, honestly."

"I've still got months to go," Christi said with a sigh. "I need to stay mobile. Everyone keeps asking if it's twins, but there's definitely only one baby in there."

"People just love to say that. How are you feeling?"

"Better," Christi replied, as Oscar handed her a glass of orange juice. "They got the sickness under control with tablets, so that helps. Just feeling huge, and a bit nervous about the end."

"I can understand that."

"So, tell me, as a doctor – how bad is childbirth really? Is it as awful as it looks on TV?"

"You don't want to ask me. I've never done it," Hannah said with a shrug. "And being a doctor in A&E, I only see things when they go wrong."

Christi's brow furrowed. "That must put you off having kids yourself."

Hannah bit her lip. It wasn't something she talked about much – people always had opinions, ones she often didn't want to hear.

The truth was, while she could imagine a husband in her future, she struggled to picture children. Seeing so many pregnancies go wrong had definitely made her think twice. And how could she manage parenting with the hours she worked? The answer was, she couldn't. So, what was the point?

"Sorry, that was a really intrusive question," Christi

said. "Blame the hormones. Just ignore me."

Hannah shook her head. "No, it's fine. You're right, though – it has put me off. I'm not sure kids are something I want, and as my mother likes to remind me, my biological clock is ticking..."

"Well, it is," came her mother's voice from behind her, startling Hannah. She hadn't even heard her come into the room.

"Yes, Mum," she said, trying to avoid an argument at the baby shower, even though she certainly knew more about fertility than her mother did.

The party was filled with games, food, and laughter. Although Hannah had never particularly wanted to attend a baby shower, she had to admit she was having fun. She and Anthony got quite competitive during a game that involved matching baby photos to adults, with perhaps the most competitive person in the room being Logan, who had teamed up with one of Christi's friends.

"Do you want kids?" she asked Anthony out of the blue as they sat in a corner eating iced pink and blue cupcakes.

Anthony licked the icing from his lips and turned to face her. "That's a big question."

"Your sister asked me," she said by way of explanation. "And I thought...well, if she asks about you, I should know the answer."

Although the reason had come easily enough, she wasn't sure it was the real reason she'd asked. Surrounded by people getting married and having children, it seemed like an important thing to know about him.

He shrugged. "I've never really thought about it much. I guess...if it happens, I wouldn't be upset. And if it doesn't, well, that's life."

Hannah nodded, taking it in. Her mother always made it seem like everyone was desperate to have children, that it was the obvious next step – but for her, and maybe for Anthony, it just wasn't in the cards. And that was okay...though perhaps not something to bring up while celebrating the imminent arrival of the Reynolds baby.

She could feel her mother watching her though, whenever she laughed with Anthony, or whenever his hand was on hers, or on her back. He had the subconscious little touches of a relationship down without seeming to really need to think about them. But every time he did touch her, her body seemed to react. Her heart would speed up, or her cheeks would flush, or she would forget what she was saying.

And that was no good at all. What was the point in knowing in her head that none of this was real, if her body acted as though it was?

And things didn't improve back at the holiday home. Not because it was awkward, but because it was so easy. Because they could chat about anything, and she would find herself smiling, laughing, losing track of time.

"If only Christi and Oscar had settled somewhere more central," Anthony said, topping up both their glasses of wine with the bottle they'd picked up at the local garage. "They seem to be the reason for all the family gatherings lately, and yet they're the opposite end of the UK from Mum and Dad."

"It is a bit of a trek," Hannah agreed. "But don't say that to either set of parents, else we'll find we have to host a lot – we're pretty central, after all."

"True," Anthony said with a laugh. "And that would

make the whole thing more stressful!"

And surely mean that the family figured out they weren't really dating. It would be obvious that she didn't have anything at his house, and vice versa, or that they weren't comfortable there.

"They seem happy though, don't they," Hannah said.

"Yeah, they do. I'm not sure their life would make me happy–"

"Nor me! Living down here is way too remote."

"But everything seems to have worked out well for them. And through them marrying, I met you, which has worked out well for me too."

He smiled over at her, and she felt like her heart might stop. She knew he only meant that the arrangement was working well for them both. And yet...

"I think I'd better go to bed," she said hurriedly, finishing her glass of wine more quickly than was probably sensible, and standing up.

"Oh, yeah. Of course," he said, blinking at the sudden change in topic. "It is getting late. Well, good night. I'll see you in the morning."

He hovered, as if he was going to kiss her on the cheek goodnight, but she slipped past him and hurried up the stairs.

She had some sort of ridiculous crush. And she couldn't let it get any further out of control.

When she climbed into bed, she sent a message to the group chat she had with her friends.

If someone wants to set me up on a blind date, I'll go on it.

She needed to find someone to actually date. Otherwise she was going to end up embarrassed and miserable.

◆ ◆ ◆

She had no idea what to wear on the date. It had been quite a while since she'd last been on a first date, and all the times she had dressed up recently, it had been for Anthony.

No, she told herself sternly. *Stop getting idiotic romantic notions in your head, Hannah Martin. There is nothing going on between you and Anthony King. You're imagining something because he's good-looking, kind, and you've spent so much time with him.*

After throwing on some jeans and a lacy white top, she applied a little make-up and headed out the door, feeling nervous. She wasn't really a fan of blind dates, but then, how else do you meet someone? She didn't fancy dating apps, and the men she met at pubs or bars weren't looking for a relationship. And that's what she wanted, she decided. She wanted something real. Not necessarily something serious right away, but someone who was open to settling down. She hated to think her mother might have been right – though the way her mum went about it certainly hadn't been – but coming home to an empty flat every night was getting a little lonely.

Perhaps some companionship, maybe even passion, would make the compromises needed for a relationship worth it.

But this was just a first date. A blind date, no less. She knew she was getting ahead of herself. At least it had been set up by Duncan from the hospital, and he understood the pressures of the job, so she hoped his friend would too.

She arrived early at the restaurant and hovered

awkwardly in the doorway, unsure whether to go in. She didn't know what the guy looked like, only that his name was Ted and he had blond hair. It wasn't much to go on, but she peered through the window, searching for any single, blond-haired men at the candlelit tables. There were a couple of candidates, so she took a deep breath and forced herself to walk in.

"Hello, I'm meeting someone," she said to the maître d'. "I think it's booked under his name – Ted."

The middle-aged man smiled, glanced at his notebook, and gestured for her to follow him.

She felt like every pair of eyes in the room was on her as she walked through the busy Italian restaurant. Was it obvious she was here on a blind date? Could everyone tell how nervous she was?

"Your table, madam," the maître d' said, gesturing to a table for two, with a candle and a rose in the centre, and a blond-haired man sitting across from it.

"Thank you," she said as Ted stood up. The first thing she noticed was that he wasn't as tall as Anthony – but that was a ridiculous thought. Why did it even matter?

"I'm Ted," he said with a friendly smile, holding out his hand. "It's great to meet you. Hannah, right?"

Hannah smiled and shook his hand. "That's me. Great to meet you too. This is a nice place."

They both sat down, and Hannah picked up the wine menu, thinking a nice glass of Chardonnay might help settle her nerves.

"The food here is pretty great," Ted said, opening his menu. "And I think it's got a nice atmosphere."

Is this his go-to first date restaurant? Hannah couldn't help but wonder.

When the waiter came to bring their drinks – wine for Hannah, and a lemonade for Ted, who said he was driving – Ted asked, "So, Duncan tells me you work at the hospital with him?"

Hannah nodded. "I'm a doctor in the accident and emergency department."

"That's a pretty full-on job," Ted said, sipping his lemonade. "Must not leave you with much time for a social life."

"Not really," Hannah replied with a strained smile, feeling a little irritated. Was her lack of a social life the most interesting thing about her job?

"And what do you do?" she asked, taking a large sip of her Chardonnay and trying not to splutter. "Duncan didn't say."

"I'm a swim instructor," he said, flexing his muscles and laughing. "Serious professionals only. I love the water – and it keeps me fit."

"That's interesting," Hannah said, annoyed at herself for not being able to think of anything more to say about being a swim instructor.

"I also DJ on weekends, you know, just as a hobby. All work and no play makes Jack a dull boy, right?"

Hannah looked down at the menu to hide her grimace. What would he think if he knew how little time she had for 'play'?

This date was starting to feel like a mistake. Conversation with Ted wasn't easy. It wasn't like...

Stop it, she told herself. *You cannot compare him to Anthony at every turn. Are you trying to sabotage this?*

If she was, she was doing a very good job of it. By the end of the night, she couldn't remember a time she'd been more bored and was desperate for the evening to end. She even considered having someone at work page her with an emergency – but Duncan would know, and what if he mentioned it to Ted? That wouldn't be fair.

"Can I give you a lift home?" Ted asked as they left the restaurant and stepped into the chilly night air.

She knew if he drove her home, she'd feel obligated to invite him in, and she didn't want to spend any more time with him, let alone even think about him staying over. So, she shook her head. "Thanks, but I don't live far. I'm happy to walk – keeps me fit," she said with a smile, since he'd made it very clear how important physical fitness was to him. He grinned and leaned in for a kiss, which she managed to divert to her cheek.

"Well, Hannah, it was lovely to meet you," he said. "I'll give you a call, maybe we can do this again some time?"

"That sounds nice," she said, knowing full well she'd be 'busy' every time he called. "It was nice to meet you too," she added politely. "And thanks again for dinner." She had tried more than once to pay or at least split the bill, but he had insisted.

"Good night, then," he said, and she hurried off in the opposite direction as quickly as possible, feeling irritated that she'd wasted an evening off. Had she sabotaged the date in her mind before it even started?

CHAPTER EIGHTEEN

Even though she told herself not to, Hannah found herself checking her phone after every shift, hoping to see a new text from Anthony.

They were just good friends, she reminded herself. It didn't mean anything. Occasionally, he would call her, or she would call him, and even with no family events on the horizon, winter turned into spring with them staying in regular contact, more than before.

She told him about her bad dates. She wasn't sure if she should, but he wasn't really her boyfriend, so what harm could it do? He was easy to talk to, and after a long day at the hospital, it was nice to come home and talk about someone else's day – the dramas in someone else's life.

All the while, she told herself it meant nothing. She would meet someone in her real life, someone who would replace her pretend boyfriend, and her parents would be happy when she did. It didn't matter that blind dating wasn't for her – she would find someone.

In April, on a rainy afternoon, she received a missed call from Anthony while at work. It surprised her because these days he knew her schedule well, just as she knew his, and they rarely interrupted each other's jobs.

Curious, she rang him back and was surprised when he answered right away. It was a workday for him too.

"Hey. Is everything okay?" she asked.

"I think so... Sorry for calling you at work. Christi went into labour two weeks early. I thought you'd want to know."

"Of course! How is she?"

"Still in labour, from what Oscar's said. I think she's okay, but they're concerned since it's a bit early. Mum and Dad are heading down there as soon as they can. They said they'll keep me updated."

"Is there anything I can do?" Hannah asked.

"I don't think so," Anthony said with a sigh. "I just... thought you should know."

"Thanks for telling me. Let me know if anything changes or if there's anything I can do."

"I will. Thanks, Hannah. Talk to you later."

She couldn't stop thinking about the phone call as she went back to work. Thoughts of Christi and how she was doing filled her mind, along with all the things that could go wrong in labour – things she'd seen herself. And then there was the fact that he'd called her. In a family crisis, it was her he wanted to talk to. That made her feel something she knew wasn't very sensible. She felt important, like she was part of his world, part of something bigger...

"You're distracted today," Eloise said as Hannah crossed out an incorrect instruction on a patient's chart for the third time and rewrote it.

"Sorry."

"What's the matter?"

Hannah sighed. "My cousin's wife has gone into

labour early. I'm just a bit worried, that's all."

Eloise frowned. "How early?"

"A couple of weeks."

"I'm sure she'll be fine. It's not like you to be distracted by family stuff at work!"

Hannah couldn't stop thinking about that, when Eloise went off to the next patient. She was right; she never let anything distract her at work. Not family, not men, not plans... And yet all day she'd been thinking about Anthony, and about Christi, and how thanks to Anthony, she was now closer to her family than she ever had been before.

And all without him really being her boyfriend.

Hannah smiled as she read the message: *Healthy baby girl, a little small but nothing to worry about. Christi doing fine.* There was a smiley face at the end of the message and a kiss too.

She was relieved that all was well with Christi. In her job, she saw people in medical emergencies all the time – yet of course, when it was someone you cared about, it was rather different. She responded quickly, saying how pleased she was, then messaged Christi to congratulate her. Then she wondered whether her parents knew what had happened. After all, they were only Oscar's aunt and uncle, and probably wouldn't have been given the news as quickly as Christi's brother had been. So she decided to call them, to let them know the good news.

She didn't realise how unusual it was for her to ring them until she heard the surprise in her mother's voice when she answered the phone.

"Hello, Hannah, is everything all right?" was the

first thing her mum said.

"Yes, it's fine. I just thought you might want to know that Christi had her baby. I wasn't sure whether–"

She was cut off by her mum's cheer of excitement.

"Oh, that's wonderful news! Early though, isn't it?"

"Yes, two weeks early. Anthony rang earlier, a little worried – but it seems everything's turned out okay."

"So, tell me everything – boy, girl? And how big?"

Hannah laughed. "I haven't got that many details, I'm afraid. A girl, and a little small but nothing to worry about is all Anthony said. But the baby's fine and Christi's fine, and that's all that really matters."

"Of course it is," her mum said with a cheerful sigh. "Oh, Joan must be delighted, having a granddaughter. And Christi's parents, too, of course."

A lump began to form in Hannah's throat. Her mother sounded so excited. She knew how much her mother wanted grandchildren. And yet, as time went by, Hannah was less and less sure she wanted children of her own.

"Would it be the end of the world if I didn't have kids, Mum?" Hannah asked suddenly. There was a long pause on the other end of the phone.

For a moment, Hannah thought her mum hadn't heard her, or was just not going to answer.

"Of course not," came her mum's words at last, and Hannah felt like she could breathe again. "It must be your decision. Yours and Anthony's… or, whoever."

The lump in her throat returned. She wouldn't be having children with Anthony. She wouldn't be marrying Anthony. Whatever happened, she felt she would be disappointing her parents. The whole point of this arrangement had been to avoid disappointing them, and yet the deeper she descended into lies, the more she felt like she was hurting them.

"You've always said how much you want grandchildren," Hannah said, unable to leave the topic alone.

"Yes..." her mum said, drawing out her response slightly. "And I do. But that doesn't mean I'm going to get them, or that you should have children just to please me."

"But what about my biological clock?" she asked, unable to just accept her mother's words at face value.

"Well, it is ticking. But that just means you need to know what you want. I've never wanted you to feel you had to have children – I just didn't want you to lose the option because you left it too late."

"Oh." It was all she could say. Her mother's response was a lot more reasonable than she had been expecting, and it made her feel terrible, like she'd been unfairly judging her mother's words all this time.

"Has something happened with you and Anthony?" her mum asked gingerly. "Have you made some decision...?"

"No," Hannah said hurriedly, shocked to find tears pooling in her eyes. "Just... thinking. What with Christi having the baby. That's all."

When the time came to attend the new baby's christening, she found herself looking forward to the drive down to Devon with Anthony. She looked forward to seeing all the people who were usually at these events, even her parents. She liked the break from the work bubble she so often lost herself in. And the drive itself – winding down south, as the roads became narrower and the scenery more beautiful – was something she enjoyed too.

She and Anthony would have coffee, and one of them would bring snacks, and they would chat about anything and everything. It was a few hours filled with laughter, something she had begun to take for granted in her life.

The church was surprisingly ornate for such a small village. Oscar and Christi clearly had many friends and family who wished to celebrate the birth of their daughter. Everyone was dressed in their Sunday best, and Hannah was pleased to note that her blue-and-white dress fit in perfectly with the other female guests.

Ivy greeted them with a broad smile, her little daughter Rose now toddling by her side. Her growth really did seem to mark the passing of time. She was a year old now, and it had been nearly a year since Oscar and Christi had married. Nearly a year since those drunken kisses with Anthony, since the beginning of this arrangement, since they had decided to lie to everyone and pretend they were in a deep, committed relationship.

Perhaps it was being in a church, but guilt rumbled in her stomach.

"She's getting so big," Hannah said with a smile at Ivy and Rose. She never really knew what to say about other people's children, but commenting on their growth seemed pretty universal.

"I know – it's going too fast. And her hair's getting so long, Alfie says she'll be rivalling me soon!" They all laughed; the little girl's locks were growing, but nothing like her mother's Rapunzel-esque hair.

"Hopefully I'll be able to plait it by next summer... for her role as flower girl." Ivy's eyes were bright with joy, and she held up a hand to show Hannah a sparkling diamond engagement ring.

"Oh wow, congratulations," Hannah said, genuinely happy for the sweet girl. "I hadn't heard you got engaged."

"It's only been a couple of days. Alfie proposed down on Blackpool Sands, my favourite beach..."

"How romantic," Anthony said, and Hannah was pleased he had commented, because if she didn't know what to say about other people's children, she certainly didn't know what to say about their engagement stories. She didn't know what was wrong with her; why didn't she know the appropriate ways to react to things like this?

Her life was filled with blood, gore, drama, and tears... When it came to happy news, she wasn't really sure what to say.

They made their way to a pew near the front, which had been saved for family, and Hannah waved at Christi and Oscar, who were at the front, baby Ava in their arms.

"Is that Alfie with them, do you know? Are they the godparents?" Hannah asked Anthony.

He glanced up from the order of service to look at the two people she was referring to next to the font. "I think Ivy and Alfie are godparents, although I guess you can have more than two... I don't know who the other man is, maybe a friend of Oscar's." The woman beside them turned, her long blonde hair swishing behind her, and Hannah heard Anthony's intake of breath.

"Oh. That's...that's Sam. She's an old school friend of my sister's."

Hannah frowned. "You know her, then?" she asked, confused by his reaction.

"Yeah. We used to date, actually. Didn't end

particularly well..."

"Oh, I'm sorry. Are you going to be okay seeing her?"

Anthony nodded and fiddled with the order of service. He laughed, but it sounded forced, as if he just wanted to fill the silence. "Yeah, of course. It was years ago. Just didn't expect to see her, that's all."

CHAPTER NINETEEN

At the christening, Hannah drank her glass of orange juice alone, watching Anthony as he laughed with Sam, an old friend of his sister's and apparently his ex-girlfriend, across the room.

They were driving back to London that evening; Hannah had an early shift the following morning, and Anthony had work he wanted to catch up on before the week truly began. So, they both agreed they wouldn't drink – Anthony hadn't minded, but Hannah didn't feel it was fair for her to have a drink when he couldn't, especially as he was the one who always drove them down to these events.

As pleased as she was for Christi and Oscar, the christening wasn't as enjoyable as the other events they'd been to. At first, she thought it was because it was a christening, and she wasn't religious, nor particularly interested in babies. Then, she thought it was because she wasn't drinking – although she'd never had a problem enjoying herself without a drink in hand before. She'd been to plenty of events where she was on-call, or working only a few hours later, and hadn't been able to drink.

But as she stood there, watching Sam giggle and

flip her long blonde hair, something else stirred in the pit of Hannah's stomach.

Something she didn't expect to feel.

Jealousy.

Everyone was busy socialising in the large living room of the bed-and-breakfast, where they'd decided to hold the party after the christening. No one was paying attention to Hannah, standing alone in a corner, trying to understand her feelings.

Was she jealous because he wasn't paying her any attention? Because, for the first time in a long time, she was alone in a corner? Or was it because of who he was spending his time with?

The fact that it was a woman. A very pretty woman. And an ex, at that.

Stop it, she told herself, forcing her eyes away from the attractive couple and watching some of the others instead. Her mum and dad were toasting the new baby, cooing delightedly over their grandniece. Ivy and Alfie were sitting together, smiling sickeningly at each other. An older man behind them held their daughter, Rose, and Hannah assumed he was Ivy's father.

It's not a real relationship, she told herself when her eyes wanted to dart back over to see what they were doing. *You can't be jealous. Just because he's attractive doesn't mean you have any right to his attention.*

But then, as she was telling herself this, anger began to grow. Because, while they knew it was a fake relationship, no one else did. And what was everyone else seeing? Anthony flirting with an ex, leaving the woman they thought was his current girlfriend standing alone, watching on.

Except she wasn't sure anyone was really paying

attention.

By the time Anthony came over, she was in a very dark mood.

"Lovely party, isn't it?" he said, with his usual handsome smile.

"I suppose so. If you want to stay the night, I can always get the train–"

Anthony frowned. "What do you mean? We agreed we were going back tonight – it's fine."

Hannah shrugged. She didn't feel she could tell him what was really bothering her, and yet she couldn't shake it off.

"Well, you just look like you're having a lot of fun..."

The frown deepened. "Are you not having fun?"

"I'm not really into babies," Hannah said, even though she'd already decided that wasn't the reason she was annoyed. "Or religion, you know..."

Anthony reached out and touched her hand momentarily, and damn it if she didn't feel a rush of warmth, even though she didn't want to.

"Me neither. You know that. But it's an opportunity to see everyone, have a laugh – isn't it?" Hannah felt like sticking out her bottom lip and saying that she was not having a laugh, but she already felt she was probably acting more petulant than was really acceptable.

"Yeah, I guess."

"Is something wrong?" he asked, his eyes searching her face. "Has someone said something to upset you?"

Hannah shook her head. "Just tired. It's fine, don't worry. Sorry for snapping."

He's not really your boyfriend, she told herself. *He doesn't have to deal with you in a jealous mood.*

Anthony took her hand then, and she jumped, a

jolt of electricity seeming to go right down her spine. She looked up into his dark eyes, wondering why he was holding her hand, why she felt this way, why she couldn't say anything...

"What a lovely day," her mum's cheery voice said, right behind her.

"Oh yes, lovely," her dad agreed. Hannah turned to smile at them, hoping the confusion didn't show in her eyes. So that was why he was holding her hand – to keep up the ruse. Of course it was. Why else would he do it?

Except, she thought as they made pleasant conversation with her parents, perhaps he needed to think about keeping up appearances a little more rather than flirting with his ex in front of everyone. After all, he was the one who'd suggested this arrangement. He should have foreseen that there might be situations where he didn't want a fake girlfriend in tow.

He and Sam spoke again before it was time to leave, and although Hannah was too far away to hear what they were saying, it didn't stop her from scrutinising their body language. She was staring at them, wondering if perhaps it was Sam doing the flirting, rather than Anthony being the one to instigate it, when Christi appeared at her side.

"Don't worry about them," she said in a cheery voice. "You've got nothing to worry about."

"Oh, I wasn't–" She cut herself off. What had she been going to say? That she wasn't concerned? Well, she knew she shouldn't be. Or that she wasn't watching them? That was a blatant lie. "He can do what he wants," she ended up saying.

Christi frowned, looking surprisingly like her brother had a little while before. "Things not great between you and Anthony?"

It took Hannah a minute to figure out how Christi had taken her words. Not, thankfully, as they had been meant – that because the relationship wasn't real, Anthony had no obligation to her.

No, Hannah rather thought it had been taken as a sarky comment, suggesting she didn't care what Anthony chose to do.

And that wouldn't help the situation, either.

She forced a smile on her face. "No, it's fine. I just mean I'm not worried – he's allowed to catch up with an old friend."

"So," Eloise asked as they ate stale cheese sandwiches in a hurry in the break room, "any developments with your hot not boyfriend?"

Hannah sighed. When had she become the sort of woman who sat around discussing her love life on her brief lunch break? And what was even sadder was that it wasn't a real love life – just a pretend relationship that had got complicated in her head when it shouldn't have.

"Still the same," she said with a shrug. "Still pretending we're dating, even though we're not."

"And what about the night you nearly slept together? Does that even get mentioned?"

Hannah shook her head. "There seems to be an unspoken agreement that we're just not going to mention it."

"You speak to him now, between these weird events where you pretend you're dating?" It was clear Eloise didn't understand why on earth anyone would pretend to have a partner. Either her parents weren't as overbearing as Hannah's and Anthony's, or she was just more sure of herself in saying that it was none of their business.

"Well..." For a while, there had been fairly regular calls and texts between them, so that when they saw each other again, it didn't feel so strange. But in the two weeks since the christening, Hannah hadn't heard a word from him. Although, to be fair, she hadn't rung him either. The drive home, after those weird feelings of jealousy, had been somewhat awkward – and she thought it might be better to leave well alone.

The door swung open, and a harassed-looking nurse gestured for her to follow. "We need you, Dr Martin, in room two. There's a bit of a situation."

Hannah dumped the remains of her cheese sandwich and rushed out the door, wondering what on earth was going on. When she'd left for her lunch break, everything had been calm and quiet.

"There's been a five-car collision," the nurse said as they walked. "They're all on their way here, but the one in room two is pregnant, and she's gone into labour. We need all hands on deck."

Hannah nodded and pushed any other thoughts from her mind. She was very good at compartmentalising her life and focusing on what was most important in the moment. And right now, the most important thing was the mother and baby in room two.

She went home straight after work that night, exhausted and in need of a good shower. There had been one casualty from the accident, but both mother and baby, as well as another patient she'd been working on, had survived. She felt positive in spite of her exhaustion.

When she got home, however, her positivity soon

evaporated. Her door was ajar – and she knew full well she'd locked it before leaving that morning. She always did. Upon closer inspection, it was clear that it had been forced, and she hesitated before pushing it open. She didn't particularly want to go in there on her own, but what else was she going to do? There was no one to come and help her.

The flat was silent, and, heart racing, she put down her bag and reached for a knife from the block on the kitchen counter. She wasn't sure she'd be able to use it, but at least if someone attacked her, she'd have some sort of weapon.

Thankfully, the weapon proved unnecessary. Whoever had broken in was long gone – as was her laptop, a few pieces of jewellery she never wore, and the fifty pounds of cash she kept in a mug on the bookshelf.

After double-checking that the flat was empty, she called the police. She doubted there was much they could do, but she was sure she'd need a police report to claim on her home insurance. With a sigh, she picked up her phone to dial. It was going to be a long night after an already very long day.

When she finally got to bed, Hannah tossed and turned, unable to sleep. Every sound outside on the busy London street sounded like it was inside her flat. She'd never felt unsafe living alone before, but right now she would have given anything to have someone to tell her there was no one else in her home. That she was safe. She'd had the locks changed and barricaded the front door to try to make herself feel better. Logically, she knew the thieves weren't likely to return. After all, she had very little of any value, and they'd already taken it. And still, she couldn't shake the feeling of fear that filled her mind and body.

In the end, she got up, turned on all the lights, and made herself a cup of tea. If she wasn't going to sleep, she might as well get out of bed. She glanced at her phone; it was only just gone midnight, but she'd been up since four. Without stopping to think, she texted Anthony, needing to hear a friendly voice: *Are you still up?*

His response was almost immediate. *Yes, been at the office for hours. You okay?*

She knew she probably ought to have rung her parents or one of her friends from work, but she didn't want to. She wanted to call Anthony, though she didn't want to think about why that was. Knowing he was awake, she hit dial, and he answered within two rings.

"Hey, stranger," he said, and she could hear the smile in his voice. She instantly felt bad for not having been in contact. She'd blamed him, thought he hadn't wanted to message, but she realised now that wasn't really fair. After all, just because he was a man didn't mean he had to take the lead. She was perfectly capable of ringing him if she wanted to – just like she was now.

"Hey. Sorry for ringing so late..."

"It's fine. I should be heading home, really, but I just want to get something straight on this case before I go to court tomorrow morning. Everything okay?"

Her voice shook a little as she spoke, and she hated herself for it. "Not been a great day. My flat was broken into."

"God, are you okay? Did they take much?"

"Not that much, and I'll be able to claim it all on the insurance... It's just..." She bit her lip. "I just feel quite vulnerable, you know? Knowing someone's been in my home."

"I know," he said in an understanding voice. "They won't be there, though. There's no way they'd stick around."

"I know," she said with a sigh. "I've checked the place several times, and the police did too, but I just can't shake the feeling."

"I get it. Somewhere you feel safe, and it's been violated. Have you got anyone who can come over?"

"It's so late. I'll be fine... I just wanted to talk."

"Of course. I can come over if you want me to – I mean, it'll take me an hour and a half, but if you need me..."

She smiled and felt her heart warm. He really meant it. He would have driven over, just because she felt scared, even though they weren't really together.

He was a thoroughly decent man.

"Thanks, Anthony. I'll be okay – but I appreciate the offer."

They stayed on the phone a while longer, until Hannah's exhaustion returned, and she found herself struggling to keep her eyes open.

"Sleep well," Anthony said as they said their goodbyes.

"Make sure you go home soon," Hannah said with a sleepy smile.

"I'll try. See you soon."

Moments after they hung up, Hannah slipped into a deep, comfortable sleep, which had seemed impossible to imagine an hour earlier.

CHAPTER TWENTY

It had been two weeks since the break-in, and she had managed to put it to the back of her mind. Work was busy, as always, and she realised she had barely had any contact with Anthony since that night when he had been so supportive. She glanced at the calendar on her phone, which she tried to keep up to date, and noticed they had a wedding of his cousin's to attend at the end of the month. She found she was quite pleased; she enjoyed attending events with Anthony, and it felt like it had been a while, especially since the christening had been less enjoyable.

She was wondering if she could get away with re-wearing the dress she had worn to Christi and Oscar's wedding, since so much time had passed, and there wouldn't be too many repeat guests at this wedding, when her phone rang. She was having a rare lazy morning at home, and she smiled when she saw who it was.

"Hey, Anthony," she answered, settling back against the sofa cushions. "I was just thinking about you." She blushed as soon as the words had left her mouth. "I mean, I saw we have that wedding coming up."

Anthony chuckled. "I like to think women can't stop thinking about me when I'm not around."

She rolled her eyes, but the smile remained on her lips. "I'm sure you do."

"How are things? Everything been okay since the

burglary?"

"Yeah, just busy. But no more issues, thank goodness."

There was a pause on the other end, and then Anthony continued.

"About my cousin Lauren's wedding..."

He sounded a little anxious, and Hannah fought the urge to interrupt and waited for him to finish.

"Do you remember Sam, from the christening?" he asked.

"Yes..."

"Well, we've seen each other a few times, since then. Just as friends...but she saw the wedding invitation, and she's really keen to go, see some of my family again..."

"Oh." Hannah wasn't sure what she was meant to say, or how she was supposed to react.

"And I thought, since this arrangement was just to keep our parents off our backs, and yours won't be there... perhaps you wouldn't mind?"

"Oh. Yeah, of course not."

"Saves you the hassle of attending..."

"Yeah, definitely. That sounds good." She was struggling to keep a lid on emotions she didn't really understand, and so she hurried to bring the call to a close. "I've got to run, work soon – speak another time, yeah?"

Once she had put the phone down, she sat and stared into space. She didn't have work until the following day, but the excuse had done what it was meant to – got him off the phone.

She swallowed the lump of emotion that had formed in her throat and tried to rationalise with herself. It was an arrangement, nothing more – and if it didn't suit, then it didn't make sense to keep it going.

Was he getting back together with Sam? She really wanted to know, and yet she knew it was none of her business. Was this the end of the arrangement entirely?

He hadn't said that it was...but then she hadn't given him much chance to speak after he'd asked if she was all right with him taking Sam.

And the truth was that she wasn't. She was disappointed, and upset, even if it wasn't fair of her to be. She'd acknowledged that she had some feelings for Anthony, feelings which ran deeper than they ought to for their convenient fake relationship...but he didn't owe her anything.

Surely it would have to be the end of the arrangement. His family would see him at the wedding with Sam, instead of her, and they would ask, wouldn't they? Or at least simply assume.

So she was going to have to tell her parents it was over with Anthony. And deal with all of their disappointment, as well as her own.

Curling up on the sofa with her cup of tea, Hannah began to wish they had never started this arrangement at all. It seemed to make things more complicated and painful than they'd ever been before.

I'm so sorry to hear about you and Anthony xxx

Hannah reread the text from Christi three times as she took a five-minute break from work. She had thought to get a breath of fresh air, clear her head and cool off a bit from the heat that seemed to have descended over London.

Grabbing her phone had been a mistake.

I'm so sorry to hear about you and Anthony xxx

So that was that then. They were over. The wedding had been the previous day, and clearly Anthony had taken Sam, and told people that he and Hannah were over.

And it hurt. Even though she knew it shouldn't.

Thanks x she responded, not wanting to say more without knowing exactly what Anthony had said.

He didn't want to talk about it, but if you do, feel free to ring. Xxx

She didn't want to talk about it either – and if she did, she couldn't speak to Christi. The fact that the relationship hadn't been real made her feelings more complicated than she could possibly explain to Anthony's sister. If she was going to talk to anyone, it would have to be one of her friends who knew about the whole scheme... But that would involve admitting that she was in deeper than she had admitted to anyone.

So she thought it was probably better to keep all her feelings bottled up until they eventually disappeared.

As she went back inside to shove her phone in her bag before returning to work, it buzzed in her hand, and she checked it one last time.

For what it's worth, I told him he's an idiot for letting you go. X

CHAPTER TWENTY-ONE

Having already dodged most of her mother's calls, when Hannah's phone rang that Friday evening after work, she knew she had to answer.

She was also fairly sure she was going to have to explain that she and Anthony had broken up – even if that wasn't truly what had happened.

It was a phone call she had been dreading, and one she had known would come.

"Hi, Mum," Hannah said, flicking the switch on the kettle and preparing herself a strong coffee. She thought she was going to need it. "Sorry I haven't called you back – things have been pretty hectic with work." It was always good to get the explanation in before Mum started guilt-tripping her for her lack of contact.

"It has been a while…" Mum said.

"Sorry."

"Well, I was speaking with my sister, and she said she'd been to see Oscar and Christi, and they'd mentioned something about you and Christi's brother no longer being an item…"

Hannah closed her eyes and groaned internally.

"Something about him attending a family wedding with someone else?"

"Yeah...things didn't really work out."

"I'm sorry to hear that, darling," Mum said, and Hannah thought the remorse was genuine.

"Thanks, Mum," she said, tears pricking at her eyes even though she wasn't sure why.

"You know, it's hard to make a relationship last when you work so many hours. He's such a nice young man, you really need to think about your work-life balance..."

Any warm feelings she'd felt towards her mother disappeared, and Hannah saw red. "It wasn't my work hours that ended things," she snapped. "And even if it was, why is the fact that he works until gone midnight most nights not being mentioned?"

"Well, Hannah, I don't think you're taking what I said in the right spirit at all. I simply meant–"

"I know what you meant, Mum. I know you want me to be married, I know you want me to have children. But I'm perfectly happy with my job, my friends, my life – I'm not going to sit here and mope because everyone else thinks I ought to."

For a moment, Mum was silent. Hannah didn't think she'd ever snapped at her like that, but she couldn't help it. Because the whole thing with Anthony, however falsified it was, did feel a little raw. And it was in a way that she could not understand or explain to anyone.

So then, to have her mother blame her, once again, for the breakdown of the relationship – when it hadn't been her choice to break up, and it wasn't really a relationship anyway – was just more than she could deal with.

"I have to go, Mum," she said, not even bothering to come up with an excuse. "I'll speak to you soon."

Without even waiting for Mum to say goodbye, she put the phone down.

She was fine. She had work, she had her friends, and it wasn't like she'd had tons of free time before to fill with social events. She'd had to make time since she had been pretending to date Anthony.

Things would undoubtedly be easier without that complication.

She didn't hear from Anthony for two weeks after the wedding. Not that she particularly expected to; their arrangement was at an end, so why should he call?

But they'd been together, albeit pretending, for a year, and for much of that, they had spoken on the phone between events. So, even though it hadn't been real, and she hadn't had to make time for him in her busy schedule, suddenly her time felt a little...empty. She worked extra hours, taking on shifts no one wanted, making up all the times she'd called in favours to get weekend days off to attend weddings or christenings or birthdays with Anthony.

But when she came home, whether in the evening, early in the morning, or not for several days, having slept in the on-call room, she felt more alone than she ever had.

This makes no sense, she told herself, trying to focus on the film she'd chosen to watch to pass the time. *He was never here, so why should I feel any different?*

But living alone no longer seemed to have quite the appeal it did before. Without anyone to text or call, she found herself sitting in the still silence of her flat, wishing away the hours until it was time to go to work again.

And then he sent a text. She hated how her heart raced at the sight of his name on the screen, and how a smile instantly spread across her face. She had never wanted to be the sort of woman whose moods were dictated by a man.

It seemed even more pathetic when that man hadn't ever really been hers.

I guess I didn't really think through taking Sam to that wedding. Sorry it's messed up our system... X

She reread it four times. He certainly hadn't thought it through if he wanted the arrangement to continue, because of course his family would think their relationship was over when he brought another woman to a wedding. Besides, word had spread now. Even if he wanted to (and she was fairly sure he didn't, if he was now with Sam again), everyone knew they had broken up. It would take far more explaining and scrutiny than either of them wanted if they were to start attending family functions together again.

It was hard to know what to write back. She didn't really want him to know she was bothered, or that she thought he had been rather hasty in throwing aside an arrangement that had been working well for both of them.

But it was up to him. This whole arrangement had been his idea, after all. He was perfectly within his rights to terminate it, even if he seemed to have done so rather accidentally.

And he was supposed to be clever. A top lawyer – and yet he hadn't managed to think that through.

It was amazing how a tall, leggy blonde could make a man lose all rational thought.

It had to come to an end eventually, she wrote in the end. *It was good while it lasted. I hope you'll be very happy.*

She didn't put a kiss on the end. She didn't mention

Sam. It was done, whatever it was; she needed to get over this ridiculous crush she had on him and move on with her life. She'd been happy before this ridiculous arrangement, she was sure – and she would be again. And if the place seemed empty, then she would find someone. She would date, she would get a friend to set her up, she would do whatever she needed to do to get back to the person she was before Anthony King.

CHAPTER TWENTY-TWO

As August came to a close, Hannah found that even work was not enough to distract her from how empty everything else in her life was. She was barely speaking to her parents, partly because she felt bad about snapping at her mother and yet was still too angry to apologise, and partly because she did not want to discuss Anthony, which she was fairly sure they would end up doing if she met them.

And so, she took on more work. Treated more patients, racked up sleepless nights, and barely took a day off.

"You're working too much, Hannah," the chief of emergency medicine said one Monday afternoon when he called her into his office. "You're a brilliant doctor, of course – we all know that. But you've been pulling more shifts than I've ever seen anyone do. You're going to be ill, or make some fatal mistake, and I can't have that."

"I'm fine," Hannah said, repeating the words that seemed to come out of her mouth so frequently. "I'm getting enough sleep, I promise."

The doctor before her frowned and pursed his lips. "There are rules, Hannah, you know that, and you've been getting around them. We appreciate all of your hard work, and you know we need good doctors – but you've got to start taking some days off."

Hannah opened her mouth to argue, but he simply shook his head. "This is not up for debate. I want to see your name on that rota far less, you understand?"

Feeling irritated, both with him and herself, Hannah nodded and scurried back to work. She knew she looked tired, but that wasn't due to working too many hours. It was due to not getting enough sleep, because even when she went home and closed her eyes, sleep didn't seem to come.

This is ridiculous, she told herself on a daily basis. *What are you doing, getting yourself into such a state over a man you saw at family functions? Over a stupid crush?*

She didn't allow herself to think about why her feelings might be so strong. That perhaps, without realising it, she had started to feel something much deeper for Anthony than mere attraction. That perhaps it was something more like...love.

She wouldn't consider it, because it couldn't be true. She had been in several long-term relationships as an adult where she had not felt love. She absolutely could not have fallen for a man she was pretending to date.

No, it was just attraction, and perhaps the added interest of him being fairly unavailable. She had not had to live with him, had never fallen out with him, had never been through any crisis with him. It was all fun and light – and that was surely what she wanted.

"You look miserable," Eloise said at lunch that day, with all her usual tact.

Hannah rolled her eyes. "Thanks."

"What's the matter? Did you mess up a procedure? Is that why Dr Ellis called you into his office?"

Hannah shook her head. "I've just been working too many hours, that's all."

Eloise let out a low whistle. "Wow, you must've been doing a lot. I've never heard them complain about anyone working too much before. So, did something happen? To make you just want to be at work?"

Hannah gritted her teeth and stared into the far too weak cup of coffee in front of her. She loved her friends, but she didn't want to be grilled on what was wrong with her. Especially when she didn't really know how to put it into words.

"Just a lot on my mind," she said vaguely, hoping Eloise would accept that she didn't want to talk about it. "Nothing major. I'll take a few days off soon, make management happy."

And so, when Oscar called her that evening, she couldn't quite believe how good his timing was.

She almost didn't answer, because she really wasn't in the most sociable of moods. But then she realised she would have the whole evening to sit in silence alone, and thought she shouldn't pass up the opportunity for some conversation if it was offered. Besides, Oscar was always pretty good at taking hints.

She didn't think he'd linger on a topic if she made it clear she didn't want to discuss it.

"Hi, Hannah. It's Oscar. How are you?"

"Good, thanks," she said, offering the easiest answer even if it wasn't entirely true. "How are you? How's baby Ava?"

She could hear him smiling as he answered. "We're great, thank you. Ava is doing well, gets bigger every day, and Christi is in her element juggling it all."

"I'm really pleased for you," she said, and she meant

it – even if she was finding it quite hard to hear about how happy people were right now. She didn't want a life with a husband and a child, she didn't think, so why did it matter if anyone else was happy with that?

"Sorry I've not been in touch for a bit. It's been manic with the summer season, the campsite, the B&B, and Ava, of course."

"It's fine, I understand – and I've not exactly been in touch, either."

"Well, I know how busy you are. And so I don't know whether this is an absolutely ridiculous question, but we've had a last-minute cancellation in the yurt on the campsite for next week. Over the August bank holiday too, and it's set to be a scorcher. Their kid's got chickenpox, apparently – can't be helped."

"That's a shame," Hannah said, wondering why on earth any of this was relevant to her.

"Well," Oscar continued, as if he'd read her mind, "Christi and I were wondering if you fancied a break down in Devon. We wouldn't charge you anything, but I know things haven't been the easiest lately, and we thought you might want to get away."

"Oh," Hannah said, rather surprised by the offer. It was the sort of thing she would normally have instantly said no to, pleading too much work. Indeed, she nearly came out with the standard excuse – well, it wasn't really an excuse. It *was* hard to get out of work. But then she thought about it, about how she really needed to take a few days off, and how they couldn't exactly complain about her being on holiday when they had said she needed a break.

Although she hadn't seen it, she'd heard that the yurt was beautiful. Anthony had stayed there with his friends and told her about it.

And if it was indeed going to be hot, it would be far more pleasant to be out of London.

"We can pick you up from the train station," Oscar said when she still hadn't responded. "And we're not expecting anyone else..." He trailed off. "That is to say, you don't need to worry about running into anyone you don't want to see while you're here."

So there was no chance of Anthony being down over the same period. Well, that was both a blessing and a curse. Seeing him would be hard and awkward, and would probably involve seeing Sam too – not to mention the possibilities for awkward questions and explanations that might arise.

And yet...she did yearn to see him, to see him smile in that way that lit up a room. But Oscar was telling her, very kindly, that he would not be there.

And she knew that was probably for the best.

"I'll need to check with work," she said, making an instant decision. "I've got a shift this evening, so I can ask them. Presuming it's not a problem...yes, I'd love to."

"Excellent," Oscar said, and she couldn't blame him for sounding surprised. She never did anything spontaneously, and she always made her plans far in advance so that she could get the time off work.

But right now...right now she really needed to get away from it all, to get out of her head and stop obsessing over a stupid man.

And if work didn't want her to lose herself there, she would just have to find somewhere else.

CHAPTER TWENTY-THREE

The train to Devon was packed, and Hannah spent half of it standing. She had booked a seat but couldn't even get down the carriage far enough to sit in it. She supposed much of the country was heading away for this sunny bank holiday weekend, the last bank holiday until Christmas. She had never marked her life by holidays before, and yet this past year had certainly been marked by events: weddings, christenings, parties, Christmas.

Once they were past Bristol, the train got a little quieter, and Hannah was able to slip into a window seat, although she was quickly trapped by an elderly gentleman with too many bags and a cane that kept falling over and hitting her knees.

She was grateful to have a seat, though, and she watched as fields and trees whizzed by, before giving way to water, sparkling in the late summer sunshine.

Perhaps she would swim in the sea while she was in Devon. She hadn't done that in years. But maybe it was just what she needed to clear her mind of Anthony once and for all.

The train station in Totnes, where Oscar told her to get off, was the smallest train station she thought she'd ever seen. Two platforms – one going north, one going south. As she did every time she came down there, she wondered how people coped without the conveniences city life offered.

Oscar was waiting by the entrance, a broad grin on his face. His skin was tanned, presumably from all the time he spent outside. He offered to take her bag before walking in the direction of his truck.

"Train okay?" he asked.

"Heaving," she answered. "I guess everyone wants to get away for a sunny bank holiday weekend."

He chuckled. "We don't get many of them, do we?" he said with a laugh.

"I bet the campsite has been busy," Hannah said as they pulled out of the station and sat waiting for the traffic lights to change. "I bet you could have re-let the yurt. I don't want to feel like I'm taking business away from you."

Oscar shook his head. "No, it was too late to book it out. We're pleased you could come – although a bit surprised you could get the time off work."

"I know. Normally, I wouldn't be able to. But I've been working a lot of overtime, so they were keen for me to take a break anyway. Your invitation came at the perfect time."

"I'm pleased. And...how are you?"

Hannah shrugged. "I'm fine."

"Mum said she talked to Aunt Mary, who said you'd fallen out, that you weren't in the best place..."

Hannah sighed. She hoped this was the most she would have to talk about her recent terrible mood. "I've just had a lot on my mind. And Mum blaming me for everything with Anthony, because I work too much, just didn't help."

"Ah," Oscar said with a knowing nod. "I don't think Aunt Mary mentioned that in her conversation with Mum."

Hannah grimaced. "No, I'm sure she didn't. It's what she always thinks. And maybe sometimes it's true. But it wasn't this time."

She couldn't tell him that the reason it wasn't true was because it wasn't a real relationship, and therefore neither of them could be offended by the other working long hours.

"No. From what I hear, Anthony probably works the same hours you do – more, possibly."

"Well, exactly. But it's never the man's fault for working too much, is it?" she said sardonically.

"I feel I need to apologise for my whole gender," Oscar said as they turned onto narrower lanes Hannah was sure she recognised from her journeys down here with Anthony.

Hannah laughed. "Well, it's definitely not your fault. And not Anthony's either, to be honest. It's my mum's expectations... I sometimes wonder what it would have been like if she'd had a son. I doubt she'd be pressing him to get married instead of focusing on his career."

After a journey through the winding roads of the southwest countryside, they arrived at what Hannah presumed was Christi's aunt's campsite in the late afternoon. She got out of the car to find the sunshine warmer than she had been expecting, and she smiled at the feel of it against her skin.

"Here we are," Oscar said, closing his door and grabbing Hannah's bag. "Christi and I don't live here, but we're only in the next village. And Christi's aunt lives in the little house just there – Olivia, you remember her?"

Hannah nodded. The kindly woman with the brightly patterned dresses was not someone she would quickly forget.

"Well, she'll be happy to give you a lift if you want one. You can walk into town if you fancy it, or down to the beach. The hill's a bit of a killer on the way back, though. I'm afraid taxis are pretty much non-existent around here unless you book in advance," he said with a wry smile.

Hannah grinned. "You know there's a reason I like living in the city. But I'm quite happy just to take it easy; I haven't had a break in a long time."

She followed Oscar onto the camping field, which was packed with tents and caravans. They didn't obscure the beautiful view of the sea, though, and she took a moment to take it all in, breathing in the sea air and trying to let go of everything weighing her down.

"This way," Oscar indicated. They passed a building with a beautiful ocean mural on it, and the waves looked so real Hannah found herself reaching out to touch them, just to reassure herself they were really done in paint.

"That's Olivia's handiwork," Oscar said, noticing her attention had been caught. "When Christi arrived four summers ago, she wanted to do all these renovations, but with no money," he said with a laugh. His eyes were warm, and it was clear the memories were happy ones.

"So I built this, and then got her aunt to paint it. Then there was a hot tub, at the top of the field, the fairy lights, the new showers...she did a hell of a lot without any money coming in."

Hannah followed Oscar up the field towards the wooden structure that would be hers for the next few nights. "She really found her feet here, didn't she," Hannah said with a smile. "And she never wanted to return to the city?"

Oscar shrugged. "I like to think she had a few reasons for sticking around."

Of course. Perhaps she had stayed for the campsite, but she had also stayed for love.

"She considered moving to Edinburgh with her parents for a while."

Hannah raised her eyebrows. "Really? From what she's told me, and what I've seen of them together, I wouldn't imagine them living together would run smoothly..."

Oscar chuckled. "No, I don't think it would have done. I think it's for the best for all of us that she decided to stay. And the campsite just gets busier every year – and now with the B&B as well, I don't think the place would cope if she decided to leave."

Hannah glanced up at her cousin. "I don't think she's going anywhere. I've never seen somebody as at home somewhere as Christi seems here."

Oscar took out a large key and unlocked the yurt. It was set slightly away from the campsite, and inside resembled a hotel room more than it did a place you would camp.

"It's beautiful," Hannah said, turning to Oscar. "Thank you, to you, and Christi and Olivia, for offering this. I think it might be just what I need."

Oscar grinned. "Well, I might be biased, but I always think Devon is the best place to be if you're feeling low, especially when it's sunny. Christi was responsible for all of this – and it's got its own wildflower garden, too, although I think everything is probably a bit brown now."

"I thought I might head down to the beach this afternoon," Hannah said, as Oscar placed her bag on the double bed. "Maybe if you could point me in the right direction? Although if I get lost, I've got no one rushing me to be anywhere." It was such a strange feeling not to have work looming over her. She had worked so much in the last few weeks, it was all she'd thought about – well, it was all she tried to think about.

She wanted to forget, and swimming in the sea seemed like a good start.

"I can take you, although I might just drop you down there and then direct you on where to go to get back. I'd better be heading off soon anyway; Ava gets fussy around now, and Christi will have her hands full checking in guests for the bank holiday weekend."

"If you don't mind," Hannah said. "Let me just grab my stuff; I'll only be a second."

On the drive down into the little town of Salcombe and one of its beaches, Oscar said, "Will you come over for dinner tonight? Christi really wants you to. She doesn't want it to be awkward, because she's Anthony's sister..."

Hannah shook her head. "It won't be awkward, don't worry." She wondered, not for the first time, whether she should have been a little more discerning with who she chose to randomly kiss in order to shut her parents up at Christi and Oscar's wedding. It was certainly more complicated that the man she had ended up pretending to date – and then potentially falling a little too hard for – was the brother of her cousin's wife.

"I'd love to come, thanks."

Oscar's ever-present smile filled his face. "Brilliant. She's invited Olivia too, so if it's okay, you can get a lift with her at about seven-ish?"

Hannah nodded. "I'll be there."

The beach was full of families with young children, enjoying the end of the summer holidays. She imagined it would be even busier once the weekend actually hit and more people were off work. It didn't matter that it was busy, though. She only needed to find a small space for herself. She'd brought a book with her, although she couldn't remember the last time she'd read one. First of all, though, she awkwardly changed into her bikini under her towel and headed straight for the water. After all, this was why she wanted to come down to the beach.

The sea was full of people – although possibly more children than adults – swimming, splashing, and shrieking. She dipped her toe in and was surprised at how cold it still was, despite the air being so warm. She didn't remember it being so cold as a child, but then she supposed memories changed, faded, and distorted. Perhaps the sea was never very warm in England.

Despite the cold, she stepped further into the water, gasping as it lapped around her knees. *Get a grip,* she told herself. Very young children in the water weren't making as big a deal of it as she was.

When she finally reached the point where the water was up to her chest, she took a deep breath and forced her shoulders under the water. The cold took her breath away, and for a moment she wondered how anyone stayed in there for more than a second. Then her body began to acclimatise, and she found it wasn't all that bad. She began to swim a weak breaststroke parallel to the shore. She couldn't remember the last time she'd swum in the sea – or the last time she'd swum at all. She was almost surprised she still remembered how, although she supposed it was one of those things you never forgot, like riding a bike.

Time seemed to pass without her really noticing, as she swam back and forth, then lay on her back, enjoying the feel of the icy cold water surrounding her head.

Yes, this was just the thing. She might not have understood why people would choose to live in Devon, but being able to swim in the sea like this was certainly a bonus. It washed away her anxieties, cleared her mind of her thoughts, and by the time she got out, she felt lighter than she had in weeks.

Up until now, she had been throwing herself into work, but it had not been the answer to her problems. No, getting away from it all seemed to be a better option. She just needed to make sure she didn't take her problems back with her when she went home.

CHAPTER TWENTY-FOUR

It was a short drive to Oscar and Christi's B&B, but Olivia filled it with happy chatter. She always seemed to look on the sunny side of life, and Hannah found her quite uplifting to be around.

"We're so lucky to have such beautiful weather for a bank holiday weekend," Olivia said as she drove.

"Really lucky," Hannah agreed. "It was beautiful on the beach today – beautiful and very busy."

Olivia chuckled. "I bet. I love the summer, but personally I'm a big fan of the beach in winter."

Hannah frowned. "Really?"

"I like to walk along it when there's no one else there – or at least, just a couple of dog walkers. I find it very peaceful... Although obviously not great for swimming."

"I have to say, I like the hustle and bustle of the city. I couldn't imagine living anywhere like this, especially in the winter." While Hannah could see how it might be pleasant to walk on the beach alone in winter once or twice, surely the benefit of living somewhere like this was that, when the weather was good, the beach was right there? And it wasn't like the weather was good very often.

Olivia grinned wistfully. "I used to think I wanted

to live in the city," she said as she turned into the road that Hannah recognised as leading to the B&B. "I thought that, with my art, a city was the best place to be. But then I came down here, and fell in love with it... Well, the rest is history."

"You couldn't imagine ever leaving?" Hannah asked.

Olivia shook her head. "I did think about it once, many years ago."

"Where were you going to go?"

Olivia sighed. "Bristol. So only a couple of hours away, but a very different way of life."

"But you changed your mind?"

Olivia drove up the steep driveway and stopped the car, yanking the handbrake on and leaving it in gear. "I did. I realised I was making the decision for all the wrong reasons."

She caught Hannah's eye and smiled. "I was going to do it for a man. Because he asked me to. But eventually, I realised I wasn't willing to compromise on what I wanted out of my life for someone else." She shrugged. "Maybe I'm selfish. But I'd lived my life until that point doing what I thought would make other people happy, and when I realised that I was the only one who would make sure that I was happy, the decision became a lot easier."

"I don't think you're selfish," Hannah said. "What happened in the end? With the guy?" As far as she knew, Olivia wasn't married. And she didn't live with anyone, either. She could very well have been widowed, or divorced – Hannah couldn't see any reason that that would have been mentioned to her.

Olivia smiled sadly. "Nothing happened. We went

our separate ways. I still see him, now and then." She opened the car door. "We'd better get in, or Christi and Oscar will think we've forgotten to turn up."

Olivia knocked on the door and then pushed it open without bothering to wait for an answer. It seemed people were not as worried about locking doors around here as they were in London. A shiver went down Hannah's spine. A locked door had always made her feel safe – and yet it hadn't really helped when thieves had broken into her flat.

They entered to the delicious smell of food cooking, and the sounds of Ava screaming.

"Christi, Oscar, it's just us," Olivia said as they walked down the corridor towards the kitchen. As well as running the grand house as the B&B, Christi and Oscar lived there, with their own section of the house locked off from the other guests.

Oscar was at the stove in the kitchen, stirring something, while Christi was pacing backwards and forwards with the baby, her curly hair escaping from the bun she'd shoved it up in. She turned and smiled as they entered, and Olivia went straight over and put her arms out for the baby.

"I'll take her, you sit down," she said.

"You don't have to, Aunt Olivia. She's in her usual bad mood, like she is every day at this time."

But Olivia just smiled. "You know I don't mind. And she usually settles with me, eventually."

Looking a little relieved, Christi handed the baby to Olivia, who began pacing up and down rocking her. The crying did seem to lessen a little, and Christi turned her attention to Hannah.

"It's great to see you," she said, pulling her into a

hug. Although she wasn't the cuddliest of people, Hannah reciprocated.

"It's great to see you too. And thanks for suggesting the break, I think it's just what I needed."

"I'll just say now that my brother's an idiot. Then I won't mention his name again."

"Agreed," Aunt Olivia said with an emphatic nod. Somehow, Ava was now lying happily in her arms, not a tear in sight.

Hannah smiled awkwardly. "Thanks." It was such a tricky area to navigate. It didn't seem fair to agree with them. He *had* called time on the arrangement, albeit possibly unwittingly, but since they weren't really a couple, she couldn't exactly feel hurt about it. Even though she felt like the injured party, she really wasn't. It was a mutual arrangement that had now come to an end.

But if she disagreed with them, stood up for Anthony... Well, then that would surely end up with them asking questions that she didn't have an answer to. No, she thought it was best to just smile and nod and move the conversation on. If they had been sensible about all this, they would have discussed the details of how they were going to handle their breakup. But they hadn't, and now she was having to deal with the questions on her own, on the fly.

Dinner was delicious, and the wine and the conversation flowed easily. Once Christi had fed the baby, and she was sleeping peacefully in her arms, Hannah found herself looking over at her cousin and his wife. They just seemed so happy. Yes, Christi looked tired, and the baby spent a decent amount of the night screaming, and the kitchen was now a mess. But when they looked at each other, there was so much love in their eyes that it almost made Hannah ache.

Was this what she wanted? Domestic bliss? She didn't think so. But to have someone by her side, someone who looked at her the way Oscar looked at Christi... Well, that wouldn't be so bad.

After an extended weekend of sun, sea, sand, late nights over bottles of wine, and lazy lie-ins, Hannah felt much more herself. Indeed, when she returned to London, she was eager to get back to work. She also knew she needed to make things right with her mum.

It wasn't fair for her mum to constantly make digs about Hannah's single status or to blame her for her relationship ending. But that didn't mean Hannah wanted to fall out with her over it.

After work, where her friends had all commented on her tan from only a few days away and how unusual it was to see her take any time off at all, Hannah caught the train to her parents' home and knocked on the door, unexpected and unannounced.

Her dad answered, a cheery grin on his face. "Hello, love. Didn't know we were expecting you."

"You weren't," Hannah said with a shrug. "I just thought I'd drop by...hope that's okay."

"'Course it is. You know you're always welcome, and we haven't seen you in a while. Come in – you're looking well."

"I, uh, went to Devon for a few days," she said, realising it was the sort of thing she'd usually have told them beforehand. But, feeling irritated, she hadn't rung them to share it. Actually, it wasn't something that had happened often in the past, so there was no real precedent.

Her dad's eyes widened in surprise. "How lovely. Over the bank holiday weekend?"

Hannah nodded, taking a seat on the familiar burgundy sofa. "Yeah. It was a last-minute thing – Oscar and Christi invited me down, and I thought I could use a break."

"Sounds very sensible, love. I'll put the kettle on. Tea or coffee?"

"Coffee, please." She bit her lip. "Is Mum in?" She wasn't sure if her mum was out, busy in the house somewhere, or had heard her voice and wanted to avoid her.

"She was just dropping something over to Mrs Mackenzie across the road. She should be back any minute. I'll make a pot of coffee; it'll be ready by the time she gets back."

Hannah didn't like feeling nervous about speaking to her mum. However strained their relationship might have been, they had never argued like they did on the phone about her breakup with Anthony. They'd never gone so long without being on good terms, even if those good terms often involved Hannah rolling her eyes rather a lot.

She fiddled with a loose thread on her T-shirt and jumped when the front door opened and she heard her mum's voice ringing through the house. "They're closing that road again, love. It's every five minutes; I just don't understand it. Can't they get all the work done in one go?" When she entered the lounge and saw Hannah, she stopped in her tracks.

"Hi, Mum."

"Hello, Hannah. Did we know you were coming? I don't remember..."

Hannah shook her head. "I just wanted to see you. I wanted to say... I'm sorry."

"Oh." Her mum's eyes widened in surprise, mirroring her dad's earlier expression.

"I still don't think some of your assumptions about my relationships are fair," Hannah continued, pushing on before she lost her nerve. "But it was wrong of me to shout at you like that and hang up. And I'm sorry." For a moment, Hannah thought her mum wasn't going to respond. She just stood there, blinking and staring.

Then tears filled her eyes, and Hannah felt terrible. "I didn't mean to upset you. I liked Anthony, that's true. And I thought maybe... But you're right. His working hours make as much of an impact as yours do, and I shouldn't forget that. I'm sorry."

They embraced – something they didn't do very often – and Hannah felt as if a weight had lifted from her shoulders.

"You'll find someone, you know. When the time is right. Someone who fits into your life the way you want it to be, and where you won't have to change everything just to make it work."

Hannah gave her mum a watery smile. "Thanks, Mum. I'm not sure though..." She thought back to what Olivia had told her about her own youthful romance – about how she'd realised she wasn't going to compromise who she was or what she wanted for anyone.

"I think my job means too much to me. I don't want to compromise on it, or feel bad about it, not for anyone."

Her mum reached out and took her hand as her dad bustled in with a coffee tray. "And one day, you'll meet someone who either makes you want to compromise, or for whom you don't need to compromise at all. It will work out in the end, Hannah, I truly believe that."

So, Hannah focused on the thing she knew she loved and trusted that her mother was right: that even though she felt lonely sometimes, things would work out in the end. She had the job she'd always dreamed of, lived in one of the most vibrant cities in the world, had friends who were always there for her, and family she could rely on – even if she wasn't always keen on their opinions.

CHAPTER TWENTY-FIVE

When the invitation to Oscar's fortieth birthday party landed on the mat by her front door, Hannah was busy at work. Autumn leaves covered the pavements, and, combined with an unfortunate amount of rain, had led to far more accidents than usual. Accident and Emergency was busier than ever, and although Hannah didn't find broken bones particularly interesting, she always relished a job well done.

She was surprised to see a handwritten envelope when she finally picked up her mail, and tore it open, wondering if some other relative was getting married.

Once she'd read it, she rather wished it had been a wedding invitation. If it had been, she could have just made an excuse about work to avoid attending; after all, that was what she had always done in the time before 'the arrangement'.

But she couldn't turn down an invitation to Oscar's birthday. Not with how close they'd become in the last fifteen months. He and Christi were her closest family besides her parents, and unless she truly couldn't get out of work, she couldn't imagine not attending.

Part of her felt sad at the thought of attending a family event without Anthony. And then she realised he would, of course, be there, being Oscar's brother-in-law, which made her even more wary.

There'd been no contact between her and Anthony since those last texts. The arrangement had ended amicably on the surface. Yet she harboured some resentment toward him for ending it the way he had – even if it wasn't fair. And she wasn't entirely sure she was over the crush she'd developed while they were pretending to date.

She groaned and poured herself a glass of wine. And, of course, he would probably be there with her. She hated her with a passion that wasn't fair, but she didn't see how it was doing anyone any harm. She did not want to turn up alone, just to see him and her together... Even if it didn't make sense. It wasn't as if he were really her ex, and she needed to make him jealous.

No, she just couldn't face going alone.

"Thanks for doing this," Hannah said to Tim for what felt like the hundredth time as they drove through the countryside toward Oscar's birthday party.

As she drove, she realised she'd never actually driven here alone before. She rarely drove at all, to be honest. Although she had a license, she didn't keep a car – there was little point in London. But for this weekend, she'd rented one, figuring it would be simpler than taking the train.

"It's fine. Michael's away for the weekend, so I'd have been on my own anyway. You know I'm always happy to help a friend in need," Tim replied.

Hannah smiled. When she'd gone to her friends asking if anyone could suggest a plus-one for her cousin's fortieth birthday party, she hadn't expected it to be so easy. But the offer of a night away in Devon at her expense had sweetened the deal.

"So, do I need to pretend we've been dating for ages or anything?" he asked with a grin.

"No," she said quickly, the memory of her last faux relationship still fresh. "You're just my date. I mean, maybe don't mention you're married, but beyond that, let's keep it simple. I just... I didn't want to go alone."

"I get that," Tim said with a sympathetic smile. "It's hard going to family events when your ex is going to be there."

Hannah sighed. "Exactly. Except... We're not really exes – it shouldn't bother me that he'll be there with someone else. I mean, it doesn't, really... It's just that we used to go to these things together, and now I don't want to go alone."

"You could have said you had to work..."

"It wouldn't feel right missing my cousin's birthday," Hannah replied, shaking her head. "Not after how much we've seen each other over the past year."

Tim was quiet for a moment, and Hannah focused on the lanes of traffic leading to Exeter.

"Can I say something? Without you biting my head off?" Tim asked finally.

"I never bite anyone's head off," Hannah said, rolling her eyes. "Say what you want."

She glanced over at him for a second. He tilted his head as if weighing his words carefully.

"You can be a bit spiky, Han," he admitted, and Hannah didn't reply to that. "But that's not what I wanted to say. I think... I think you fell deeper for Anthony than you're admitting – to us or to yourself."

"That's ridiculous," Hannah said, scoffing. "It was

all pretend. Then he rekindled something with an ex – that's all."

"You can say that," Tim replied gently, "but none of us believe you."

"What?"

"We saw you when you were with him, and we've seen you since things ended. Whether or not the relationship was real, I think you felt something real. I think maybe you still do…"

It was a lot to think about. He didn't bring it up again, but her mind kept returning to it. She'd admitted her feelings to herself, hadn't she? She knew she had a crush on Anthony. She was dealing with it.

But…what if it was more than a crush? What if Tim was right? What if she had real feelings for Anthony…and all they'd ever had was a fake relationship?

They arrived at the little pub where Hannah had booked rooms for them, and she clumsily parallel-parked the rental car in a tight space.

Oscar had offered her a room at the B&B, but she preferred separate rooms, to have her own space and because it wasn't fair to Tim's partner to share a room with her for the night.

The pub had the added benefit of being within close walking distance of the village hall where the party was held, meaning they could both have a drink without worrying about finding a ride back. She knew she'd need a drink – to face her family, deal with seeing Anthony, and mull over what Tim had said.

She wore her favourite little black dress and spent longer on her hair and makeup than she had in ages. She just wanted to look nice, she told herself. It was important to make an effort.

And yet...deep down, she knew it was because she would be seeing Anthony again after so long.

She was sure he'd be polite, but doubted he'd have eyes for her at all with his new girlfriend by his side. Well, old new girlfriend.

Still, she wanted to look her best.

She met Tim downstairs in the bar, and he wolf-whistled, making her blush.

"He won't be able to take his eyes off you," he said with a grin. "I don't think I've ever seen you so dressed up, you look amazing."

She fiddled with the strap of her handbag, feeling a surprising surge of nerves. She didn't even bother denying that she'd dressed up for Anthony. "Thanks, Tim. For everything."

"I told you, don't worry about it. Now, shall we?" He offered her his arm, and she giggled as she took it. "You shall go to the ball."

The village hall was decorated with more balloons than Hannah could count, many bearing the number '40' in large print. A band was setting up on stage, and a bar operated from the corner of the room. Few people had arrived yet, but Oscar spotted her immediately and made a beeline for them.

"Happy birthday, Oscar. Officially old now..."

Oscar chuckled. "In a few years, you'll be right here with me."

"This is Tim," she said, belatedly realizing she hadn't introduced her date. It felt odd to think of Tim that way. "Oscar, this is Tim – Tim, my cousin Oscar."

They shook hands, and Tim wished him a happy birthday. Hannah couldn't help glancing around for Anthony, but there was no sign of him yet. She saw

Christi talking in the corner with Mrs King, and her aunt chatting with Mr King. She also spotted Logan, Anthony's brother, at the bar, and when he caught her eye, she waved politely.

"Hannah, darling," came her mum's voice. Hannah turned to smile and hug her, relieved they'd mended things before tonight.

"That's a lovely dress, dear," her mum said, giving her an appraising look. "Have I seen it before?"

Hannah resisted reacting to the implied dig about her not owning many clothes. "Thank you, Mum. I'm not sure, possibly. Mum, this is Tim – we work together at the hospital."

Hands were shaken all around, and then Oscar drifted off to make the rounds. "Let's get a drink," Hannah murmured to Tim, who followed her to the bar.

"Hannah! Good to see you," Logan said, pulling her into a hug. She never understood why everyone was so hug-happy at events like these, even before they'd had a proper drink.

"Good to see you too." She managed to stop herself from asking the only question on her mind: Is Anthony coming?

But she didn't need to. Logan's eyes brightened as he looked toward the doorway. "Ah, there he is," he said, striding over to greet his brother. "Good to see you! You've been AWOL lately."

Hannah focused on ordering a drink, her pulse quickening at the sound of Anthony's deep voice. "Been crazy with work," Anthony said. "But it's good to see you too."

"Let's get a drink," Logan said, and Hannah braced herself for the rush of emotions she knew would hit when he spotted her.

"Hannah!" His voice was as warm and friendly as ever. She turned with a full smile; she really was glad to see him, though it stung too. She thought she was finally beginning to understand why...

"Hi, Anthony," she replied, trying to remember that, to everyone else, they were exes, not friends.

But he didn't seem to care. He pulled her into a hug, and the smell of his aftershave sent her heart skittering. And, strangely, she didn't mind the hug.

Beside her, Tim cleared his throat, and when they broke apart, Hannah introduced them, blushing without fully understanding why. "Anthony, this is Tim. Anthony is Christi's brother," she explained to Tim, though he hardly needed it. She was sure that's why he'd interrupted – to make his presence known.

She couldn't help but notice there was no sign of Sam coming in behind him. Then again, she knew Christi, and the rest of the family too; perhaps Sam had been waylaid by one of them on the way in.

"Can I buy you a drink?" Anthony asked, flashing that handsome smile at both of them.

At that moment, the barman handed Hannah her glass of wine and Tim's beer.

"We're sorted, thanks," she said, handing Tim his drink.

"Maybe later then, yeah?" he said, his eyes raking up and down her body. "You look great, Hannah."

She didn't want to, but Hannah knew her cheeks had flushed bright pink. "Thanks," she managed to squeak before disappearing over to the table with Tim. She didn't want to make a fool of herself, looking like some lovesick puppy – especially once Anthony's girlfriend showed up.

"You like him," Tim stated assertively, taking a swig of his beer. "In fact, I think you might love him."

"Shut up, Tim," Hannah hissed, seeing Christi heading in their direction. "You don't know what you're talking about."

But just before Christi was in earshot, Tim grinned and muttered, "He wants you. Surely you can see that by the way he looks at you."

Tim's words, both in the car and after the encounter with Anthony, stayed with her all night. Could he be right? Could Anthony feel something for her?

And had she truly fallen...in love with Anthony?

It didn't make sense. And yet she was becoming more and more concerned that that was exactly what had happened.

CHAPTER TWENTY-SIX

They ate the food, danced to the cheesy DJ, and drank more wine than was sensible – and yet still she saw no sign of Sam. Feeling emboldened by that, she approached Anthony while Tim was finding the bathrooms.

Anthony was sitting alone, a piece of birthday cake untouched before him, his dark hair looking a little tousled, as though he'd been running his hands through it.

"You can buy me that drink now, if you like," she said with a cheeky grin that was entirely due to the numerous glasses of wine she had already consumed.

He looked up at her, beamed, and gestured for her to sit down opposite him.

"My pleasure. White wine?"

She nodded and waited while he went over to the bar, where a short queue had formed. She saw Tim looking for her and raised a hand, but then jerked her head towards the bar, and he got the message. She knew he'd tease her for it later, probably come out with some more wise words about why she was such a fool when it came to this man, but in that moment, she didn't care. She wanted to sit with him and talk, alone, just for a little while. One more time. It had been so long since she'd seen him – well, so long considering the frequency with which they'd met up for more than a year.

When Anthony returned with the drinks, she could feel her pulse quickening, and she bit her bottom lip, unsure of how to act around him.

"It felt weird coming to this without you," he said, sliding her glass of wine across the table towards her.

"Where's Sam?" She couldn't stop herself from asking.

"Ah," he said, looking down at the table and fiddling with the label on his beer bottle. It was hard to be sure because of the low lighting, but she thought he might be blushing in embarrassment.

"Did you not get back together with her? I thought that was why you wanted to end the arrangement..."

"It was," he said, drawing out the last syllable. "We did get back together...but I'm afraid I was a bit of a fool about it all – ending the arrangement, and, without much thought, getting back with Sam..."

Hannah frowned. "What made it foolish?"

He met her eye and smiled ruefully. "Well, we broke up the first time because she cheated on me. On several occasions..."

"Oh..."

"And, as it turns out, a leopard really does never change its spots."

"I'm really sorry, Anthony," she said, finding to her surprise that she meant it. She wasn't particularly sorry that he had broken up with Sam, but she *was* sorry he had been hurt.

She reached out and took his hand, just for a moment, and then pulled it back. They'd held hands all the time while they were pretending to date, and for a moment she'd forgotten that anything was different. But of course it was. To everyone around them, they were a former couple, and her holding his hand would certainly invite questions.

"I'm glad I found out when I did," Anthony said with a shrug. "Although I could have done without walking in on them, I must say."

Hannah winced at that comment. Certainly not a pleasant way to end a relationship.

"But at least we didn't get serious or anything before I found out. I'm sorry I messed up our arrangement, though. I lost my head like a stupid seventeen-year-old all over again–and left you to answer all your parents' questions."

Hannah couldn't help trying to cheer him up. "I'm used to disappointing them, don't worry."

But at that he just gave her a sad smile. "I don't think you disappoint them, Hannah. I've heard your mum talking about you to everyone at these events. Sure, she likes to go on about marriage and babies, but she always leads with the fact that you're a doctor."

Hannah sat up a little straighter, surprised by that information. "Does she?"

Anthony nodded. "Every time. And if it makes you feel any better, I've had a right earful from everyone in my family about being a fool for letting you go," he said with a grin. "My sister especially – but she wasn't the only one."

Hannah sipped her wine, the alcohol loosening her tongue. "I'm not sure we really thought the arrangement through enough, anyway," she said with a shrug. "All these overlapping family relationships, events where we know everyone. It was bound to come to an end sometime, and there were always going to be awkward questions. I'm not sure we could have ever dissolved it without upsetting somebody."

What she didn't admit, what she never planned to admit, was how much it had upset *her*.

"Maybe you're right," Anthony said with a shrug. "Maybe we should have thought more before you grabbed me and kissed me." There was a twinkle in his eye as he said it, and Hannah reached across the table and batted him gently on the arm.

"Hey! I was only suggesting the night. You were the one who wanted the arrangement..."

He held his hand to his chest in mock pain. "You wound me, thinking I'm just a one-night-stand kind of guy."

They were in peals of laughter when Christi came over, a quizzical grin on her face.

"You two are getting on very well," she observed.

"We're friends," Anthony said. "That's not changed, has it, Hannah?"

Hannah shook her head confidently. "No. Definitely not."

But could she cope with just being friends with him? Just seeing him occasionally at family events – when, eventually, one or both of them would surely have partners to attend with?

CHAPTER TWENTY-SEVEN

She didn't spend the whole evening with Anthony, though she did find her eyes searching for him now and then. She almost regretted bringing a date – not because things between her and Tim were romantic, but because she felt guilty leaving him for too long with a group of people he didn't know.

Mum and Dad came over and chatted, as did Alfie and Ivy, and overall, it was a fairly pleasant evening. Not as much fun as the ones she'd spent with Anthony, she had to admit, but that wasn't a negative reflection, just a difference.

The next morning, they left by ten, both needing to get back for overnight shifts. Hannah felt a little hungover, regretting the amount she'd drunk, but hoped that strong coffee and a large bottle of water would help her feel normal again.

"So, he's single then," Tim said as they joined the motorway.

"Yeah, I guess so," she replied, though she had been trying not to dwell on the thought.

"What will you do about it?"

Hannah sighed. "Nothing. Because what can I do? If I admit to him that, yes, I might feel something more, and then he says he doesn't... Well, that would be terrible. And if we did try dating, how on earth would we explain it to our families? They think we were in a relationship for over a year and then split up. It's all just too complicated. Better left alone, I think."

Tim tutted. "I think you're being ridiculous. No, hear me out. You like him – you've even admitted it to yourself. And from the way he looks at you, I think he likes you too."

"But there's no way of knowing," Hannah countered.

"Of course there isn't. There never is. That's just dating, you have to put yourself out there. If you only ever made a move when you're one hundred per cent sure someone reciprocates your feelings, well then..." He glanced over at her. "You'd probably have very few relationships."

"That's not why I haven't dated much," Hannah said indignantly. "I'm busy with work; you know that. You sound like my mother."

"I'm not having a go, Hannah. I know you work long hours – but doctors do have relationships, you know."

She rolled her eyes but said nothing. Clearly, he was yet another person who thought she was sabotaging herself rather than having legitimate reasons for being single. Yes, she could put herself out there and tell Anthony what she felt, but if he didn't feel the same way, how awkward would it be? She couldn't avoid every family event he attended, just because she was embarrassed.

Her phone, connected to the car's Bluetooth, rang then, breaking the awkward silence between them. She glanced at the screen and saw that it was Christi calling. She wondered if she'd left something at the party – why else would Christi be ringing so soon after they'd just seen each other?

Hitting the answer button, she said, "Hello? I'm driving, so you're on speaker."

"I thought I should ring you," Christi said, her voice sounding a little shaky. "I know you and Anthony aren't together anymore, but you still seem like friends."

"Christi, what's happened?" Hannah asked, alarmed by the emotion in Christi's voice. She pulled into the slow lane to better concentrate on the phone call.

"Anthony had an accident on the way home. Wrote his car off."

Hannah's heart began to race. "Is he okay?"

"I've not seen him," Christi said with a sniff. "They're taking him to Bristol, we're on our way now. I don't think, from what they've said, that it's life-threatening, but I haven't been able to speak to him. I just thought you should know…"

"Yes, definitely," Hannah said, her heart pounding as she tried to make out the upcoming sign indicating how far away Bristol was. Could she just turn up at the hospital? She didn't really care whether it was acceptable or not – she needed to see for herself that he was okay. Besides, she was a doctor; she might be useful.

"I've got to run, Hannah; someone's on the other line."

"Okay, keep me informed. I'm sure he'll be okay," Hannah said, trying to reassure herself as much as Christi.

When the call ended, Tim reached over and covered her hand on the gear stick. "It'll be okay," he said. "Don't panic. You heard what she said – there's no reason to think it's anything life-threatening."

"I've got to go and see him," Hannah said, her mind made up. "I'm sorry. I just... I can't leave him there."

The sign ahead told her there were only fifteen miles left until Bristol.

"I understand," Tim said. "Shall I change the sat nav so we can head straight there?"

Hannah shook her head. "I don't know how long I'm going to be. I don't want to mess up your night shift. I'll have to ring in sick." She never called in sick – not even when she probably ought to – but this was urgent. "Would it be awful if I dropped you at the train station? I'll pay for your ticket, of course. I'm really sorry; I know this whole weekend..." She trailed off.

"It's fine," he said in a slow, soothing voice. "If you're sure. I can come with you."

She shook her head again, her hands trembling slightly on the steering wheel. She didn't want to worry about how long she was keeping someone else waiting. She wanted to focus entirely on Anthony, even if she wasn't his girlfriend.

"Okay, then. I'll set the sat nav for the station."

It all took longer than Hannah wanted, but eventually, she found a parking space in the multi-storey car park of the hospital on the outskirts of Bristol and hurried into Accident and Emergency. She was relieved to see Christi and Anthony's parents in the waiting room. She wasn't sure how much information she'd have been able to get from the staff – at least not without lying about who she was. And it didn't feel right to claim she was his girlfriend when she wasn't.

"Hannah," Christi gasped, hurrying towards her.

"You came!"

"I had to. I hope I'm not intruding."

Christi shook her head. "Not at all. We haven't seen him yet... They're talking about concussion and broken bones, but they said he's stable. I just don't understand why we can't see him."

"He's probably having x-rays," Hannah said, taking a seat on a hard plastic chair alongside Christi. So many times, she'd been the doctor on the other side, not informing a patient's family until there was a spare moment to do so. She'd never quite realised how painful the waiting could be – not until now, sitting and worrying about a man she shouldn't care so much about.

"I don't understand why he hasn't texted or called us," Mrs King said, pulling out her phone for what must have been the hundredth time. "If he was okay, he would have let us know, I know he would."

"He might have lost his phone in the accident, or it might have been broken." Hannah knew these were plausible explanations for the lack of contact, but they didn't calm her any more than they seemed to calm his family.

"Where's Oscar?" Hannah asked Christi, desperate to fill the time.

"He stayed at home with Ava. I didn't think this was the right place for her... Especially as we don't know how long we'll be here."

Hannah nodded. It was a good call – the waiting room wasn't particularly large, and a screaming baby would have only heightened everyone's nerves, Christi's included. Not to mention the increased infection risk in a hospital.

"I expressed enough for a few hours, and he's got

formula if he needs it."

Christi's hands were shaking on her lap, and Hannah reached out to take them. "It'll be okay," she said, more confidently than she felt. "The waiting is the hardest part."

"Thank goodness, you're here," a voice said. They all looked up to see the blonde figure of Sam hurrying towards them. "I got here as fast as I could."

Hannah looked at Sam, then back at Christi, her eyebrows raised.

"I thought everyone ought to know," Christi said with a shrug. Hannah wondered if Christi knew the reason Sam and Anthony had broken up the first time. But now wasn't the time to bring it up, so Hannah forced a friendly smile while Mr and Mrs King explained what little they knew.

In the anxious waiting, Hannah couldn't help but wonder why Sam was there. Who cheated on someone and then came to their bedside? But then again, people were probably wondering the same about her: who broke up with someone and then turned up at the hospital?

A nurse came out, glanced around, and then walked over to their group. "Mr and Mrs King?" he asked.

"That's us," Anthony's parents said, standing up.

"You can come with me to see your son before they move him upstairs."

Mrs King grabbed her handbag and quickly followed the nurse.

"Is he–" Christi began. "I'm his sister. Is everything...?"

"He's bruised and battered, and it'll take a while for him to recover, but there's nothing life-threatening to worry about," the nurse said with a smile. "You can all see him soon, but for now, just his parents, perhaps?"

Relief flooded through Hannah as they walked away. He was okay. She wondered if she ought to leave now that she knew that, but she couldn't bring herself to. She needed to see him, no matter how awkward the waiting room felt with Sam.

"Well, that's good news, isn't it?" Christi said, her voice full of relief.

"Excellent news," Sam agreed.

"Such a relief," Hannah added.

"Don't feel you have to stay, Hannah," Sam said in an icy tone. "We can take it from here."

Hannah bit back the retort she wanted to make. "I'm fine, thank you. But if you want to leave..."

Sam shook her head. "No, no, I want to be here to make sure Tony is okay."

"Well, I'll stay and make sure Anthony is okay before I go," Hannah said, while an awkward-looking Christi sat between them.

CHAPTER TWENTY-EIGHT

After ten long, quiet minutes, Christi's parents came and called her in, and she hurried off to see her brother. Hannah wondered if Logan was on his way or whether he had already got home and was in the middle of a shift when the accident happened, so perhaps didn't even know yet.

"What are you doing here?" Sam asked as soon as Christi was gone.

Hannah's eyes widened at the sudden, blunt question. "Christi told me about Anthony. I wanted to make sure he was okay," she said, confused by the question.

"I know. I know your relationship was entirely pretend – so I'm really confused as to why you're here."

Hannah bit the inside of her lip. She didn't really know what to say to that. She hadn't thought of the possibility that, while dating Sam, Anthony might have told the truth. Of course he would have. Now, even though they were broken up, it seemed Sam was keen to get Hannah off the scene, and possibly out their secret relationship to Christi, her parents, and everyone else they knew.

It was not how she wanted it to come out. In fact,

she'd rather it didn't come out at all.

"And I know you cheated on him," Hannah said, deciding to fight fire with fire. "So I'm wondering why you're here, too." She did not confirm or deny Sam's comments about the relationship being pretend. At least that way, she couldn't accidentally refute something Anthony had said. Lies really could get complicated...

Sam had the decency to blush, but the anger in her eyes did not fade. "That was a misunderstanding," she said airily. "And none of your business."

"Well, I'm not going anywhere," Hannah said, folding her arms and leaning back on the uncomfortable plastic chair.

"I could tell them all your secret..."

"And I could tell them you cheated on their precious son," Hannah said with a shrug. She didn't really feel as confident as she sounded, but she was not going to be bullied out of the hospital by anyone – especially not this woman.

More silence followed, and then Christi emerged from wherever they were treating Anthony, a teary smile on her face. "He really is going to be okay," she said, the relief in her voice palpable. "I know what they said, but I didn't believe it until I saw him."

"That's wonderful," Sam said.

"Great news," Hannah agreed. That was what was important – that Anthony was going to be okay, not one-upmanship with Sam.

"He wants to see you," Christi said as her parents exited to join them, "Hannah."

Hannah nodded, her heart racing inexplicably, and followed the direction Christi pointed in, not looking back at the surely venomous look Sam was giving her. *He wants me. Me,* Hannah thought, even though she knew she was being silly.

He was in a bed behind a curtain, but it was half open, and she could see, even from a distance, how pale he looked.

"Hey," she said with a soft smile. "How are you doing?"

He caught her eye, smiled, and then winced in pain. "I've been better," he said with a shrug. "There was no need for everyone to come rushing here, though... I feel like a right idiot."

Hannah sat beside him and gently laid her hand over his as though it was the most natural thing in the world. "You were in an accident, Anthony. We want to be here. But what happened?"

He sighed. "I misjudged my timing, didn't realise a lorry was going to stop, smashed into the back of it. No one else was hurt, thank God – but I'm sure my car is written off."

Hannah was sure Christi had mentioned something to that effect, but she did not confirm it. That could be dealt with later. "Don't worry about that now. I chatted with a doctor on the way in – it sounds like you got off lightly, all things considered."

Anthony nodded and then once again winced at the pain the movement caused. "Yes, I think I did, although I'm in a hell of a lot of pain."

"You're bound to be. You've got a broken leg, broken arm, possible concussion, and a couple of broken ribs. Do you want me to ask for some painkillers?"

Anthony shook his head. "They said they'd give me some when they put the casts on. I'll wait..." He turned his hand under hers and gave it a gentle squeeze. "Thanks for coming, Hannah. I really appreciate it."

She didn't know how to convey that she was happy to be there, that she wanted to be there, that she wanted to be by his side... And anyway, he didn't need to know that right now. He possibly never needed to know that.

"I'm not the only one here, you know," she said, raising her eyebrows and trying to change the subject slightly.

"Yeah, Dad mentioned," Anthony said darkly.

"She wanted me to leave. I have to tell you, she's threatening to tell everyone that our relationship wasn't real."

Anthony groaned, and Hannah wondered if she should have kept that information to herself. But she didn't think it was fair for him to end up blindsided if his parents started questioning him about it.

"I knew telling her was a mistake. She was really jealous, for some reason, about you... That you'd be at events we went to... So I told her." He tried to shrug, but the movement turned him a sickly green, and he didn't complete the action. "I don't really understand why she was jealous when she was already out there finding someone new. Don't know why she's here either, to be honest. I have no interest in seeing her. This day's been bad enough."

"You don't have to see her. And if she tells them – well, it was bound to come out eventually. We can weather their disappointment, I'm sure."

A nurse came in to check his vitals, and then his parents reappeared, without Christi this time. Hannah thought she should let go of Anthony's hand to avoid any awkward questions for him, but he kept a tight hold of it, and so it remained on the white starched sheets of the hospital bed, clasped together with his.

"The doctor doesn't think they'll keep you in very long, Anthony," his mother said, clicking her tongue. "Seems a bit ridiculous to me, but there you go. They'll get you patched up, make sure you haven't got a concussion, and then you'll be home in the next couple of days."

Hannah wasn't surprised... There wasn't enough room in hospitals for patients who didn't need active treatment.

"I'd rather be at home," Anthony said. "Don't worry about me, Mum, I'll be fine."

"You will not be fine," his mother said with a sigh. "You've got multiple broken bones, Anthony. You cannot possibly go home and live on your own – not for the first few weeks, at least."

Anthony shook his head, even though it obviously pained him to do so. "A few days, maybe, but not weeks. That's–"

"You're going to struggle on crutches with a broken arm, son," Mr King said.

"Well, yes, but–" Anthony said, clearly searching for any way out of this.

"It's all settled; you don't need to worry. You'll be signed off sick and come back to Edinburgh with us. We can make sure you're back on your feet before you go home on your own."

Anthony looked at Hannah, horror in his handsome dark eyes. She couldn't blame him – she'd be horrified too at the thought of having to live at home again with her parents for weeks on end. Especially without even having a break to go off to work. It didn't bear thinking about.

"I really don't think–" Anthony began, but his

mother was having none of it.

"You need taking care of, son. And we want to do it."

Anthony's grip on her hand grew tighter, as he clearly saw his independence fading away. And then, without thinking, Hannah piped up, "He can come and stay with me."

Six pairs of eyes were instantly upon her.

"Hannah, I couldn't, it's–"

"It's fine," Hannah said, cutting over Anthony. "I'm a doctor, after all. And if you stay with me in London, when you're ready to go back to work, it's not that far away." Plus, it would save him having to move in with his parents – something which she certainly wasn't going to say in front of them but which she was sure he appreciated.

"Look here," Mrs King said. "While we appreciate the offer – of course we do – you two aren't even together. And from what Sam has just told us, you never even were…although I don't fully understand that."

Once again, Hannah and Anthony's eyes met, both widening in horror. So she had spilled the beans… And now was the moment of truth.

"She's bitter because we broke up, even though she was the one who cheated," Anthony said quickly. "Just ignore her, please. I don't know why she's here."

"I told you," Anthony's mum said to his dad. "She can't be trusted, that one…"

"And whether or not Hannah and I are together, she is here. And if you're really sure about the offer…" He looked up at her.

"I am," she said, more sincerely than she had expected. "I'll have to work, of course – but we can figure it out."

"See, she'll have to work, it doesn't make sense after all," Mrs King said, clearly seeing the chance of having her son move home slipping from her grasp.

"Mum, I appreciate you offering, but we all know you and Dad are going to be working too. And I'm nowhere near work or my flat. It doesn't make sense. I'll stay with Hannah – until I'm okay to be on my own. And that's the end of it," he added, as his mother tried to argue.

Having three lawyers in the family certainly made arguments exhausting.

CHAPTER TWENTY-NINE

Hannah was pleased she had arranged to borrow a wheelchair from the hospital at the same time she went in to ask for a few days of annual leave. Thankfully, due to her exemplary record, her leave was granted without much question – and if her friends were nosy about why she had to take care of her fake ex-boyfriend, they didn't push the point too much.

No, she was especially pleased with the wheelchair because Anthony's dad had been right: he wasn't having much luck managing crutches with a broken arm. He could just about get by indoors, taking it slowly, but the wheelchair made things much easier.

However, that didn't stop him groaning, as though it was unnecessary, when she pulled the rented car up outside her block of flats and rushed around to retrieve the wheelchair from the boot.

"It'll be loads easier, Anthony," she said in a no-nonsense voice. "And besides, I don't want you hurting yourself any more by falling over. I'm the doctor, remember."

He sighed but allowed her to help him into the wheelchair and push him into the lobby, straight into the open lift that would take them up to her second-floor flat.

It felt strange to have him there, considering he had never been to her flat in the year or so they had 'dated'. His parents had packed a suitcase for him from his house, which was still in the car, but she would have to fetch that later. She hoped she hadn't made a mistake taking this on. She was happy to take care of him; she enjoyed spending time with him. And with a few days of annual leave to make sure he was settled, she hoped he would be all right on his own while she worked, at least until he was ready to go back to his house.

"Do you want a drink?" she asked, flicking the kettle on.

"Coffee, please," he said, shuffling himself from the wheelchair onto the sofa. "The stuff in the hospital was awful."

Hannah laughed. "It always is, unless you can get the stuff from the doctors' lounge. That's usually better. We can't survive without caffeine."

"I haven't thanked you properly," he said as she handed him a mug of coffee to his unbroken arm, then sat down beside him. "This is a hell of a lot to do for someone. But I couldn't have survived a week with my parents, let alone more..."

"I'm happy to rescue a damsel in distress," Hannah said with a chuckle.

"But seriously, it means a lot. I know I messed up our arrangement and jumped stupidly into...whatever that was with Sam, but I'm really glad we're friends. And that you're a good enough friend to be willing to do this." He gestured to the wheelchair and his broken limbs. "I could have forced Christi or Logan to step in..."

"Christi's got a tiny baby to look after, I'm not sure she could manage a broken brother as well," Hannah said with a laugh. But he was right – he could have asked Logan. And his brother probably would have done it. Yet...she was glad to be the one to do it.

Even if they were only friends.

Even if she needed to put to bed whatever feelings she still had, once and for all.

Tim had been wrong when he said Anthony wanted her – because hadn't he just said he was glad they were friends? Friends...and nothing more. She would be silly to complicate things again.

It was nice having a decent relationship with her extended family; going to family events and actually enjoying them. She didn't need to ruin all that with awkwardness. Or have to explain it all to her parents or Christi. Hopefully, Christi and the rest of the Kings believed Anthony when he said Sam was just bitter about the breakup. They didn't need another reason to suspect their relationship had, in fact, been fake.

When it came time to go to bed, Hannah helped Anthony into her room, and it was only then that he seemed to realise she only had one bedroom.

It was central London, after all, and she had been single for a long time. What need did she have for more space? Especially with how much it cost.

"I'm sleeping on the sofa," she said quickly, noticing the way he glanced at her, his eyebrows raised. Even that made her blush, remembering that time they had shared a bed...and what had nearly happened.

"I can't let you do that," Anthony protested.

"I'm hardly going to put you, with your broken limbs, on the sofa and take the bed myself," Hannah said with an eye roll. "It's fine – I've already got blankets and pillows out there. And I've slept on it plenty of times when I was too exhausted after work. Don't worry about it."

"It doesn't seem very fair..."

"It's fine. I offered, remember? You just get a good night's rest. We may be in central London, but it's got to be quieter than a hospital ward."

As she lay on the sofa, trying to sleep, she couldn't help but think about the fact that he was only on the other side of her bedroom door. She had helped him into his pyjamas – although, thankfully, he could use the bathroom on his own – and she realised she hadn't really thought about how intimate it would be to look after him during his recovery.

They had held hands before, kissed, and that night in the bed...well, they had very nearly done a lot more. But all of it – or nearly all of it – had been fake. Part of the ruse designed to make their lives better.

This was different. This was real.

No one was watching. She didn't need to prove anything. She just wanted to be there for him...

She turned over and groaned into her pillow. If she'd thought having him here would somehow help her get over the stupid feelings that had grown, she was beginning to realise she had been sorely mistaken.

How's it going with the hot lawyer at your mercy? Eloise's text message read, and Hannah couldn't help but smirk before rolling her eyes and responding:

I make his meals, we watch telly – nothing romantic, I promise you.

And it wasn't romantic; she was telling the truth. Yet it was the most intimate she'd been with another person for a long time. It was rather nice to wake up and have someone else in the flat. Or to go to bed knowing she wasn't entirely alone.

But things between them had remained simple, friendly, and fun – until the night he suggested they watch a film in her room, since it was more comfortable for him to raise his leg in bed than awkwardly propping it up on the sofa.

It had seemed like a good idea until she realised that, of course, the only place to sit in her bedroom was the bed. And that put her rather closer to Anthony, and the delicious way he made her feel, than she thought she ought to get.

They started by sitting upright, popcorn between them and plenty of space to spare. But by the time the film was halfway through, the popcorn was long gone, and both of them had slid down on the bed, the space between them slowly disappearing.

Hannah's eyes began to drift closed before the credits rolled, and she knew, in the back of her mind, that she needed to get up, go make her bed on the sofa, and remove herself from the warmth and comfort of lying beside Anthony.

She forced her eyes open when she heard the film ending and saw Anthony looking just as drowsy, his good arm behind his head, propping it up slightly.

"Night, then," she said, pleased that she'd already helped him into his pyjamas before they started the film and had put hers on too. She was too tired to think of anything else. "Here, let me get the duvet out from under your cast..."

She tugged at the duvet to move it enough to cover his body, then stifled a yawn. "I'll see you in the morning."

He turned his head, and as his eyes fluttered closed, he murmured, "Stay."

When she woke the next morning, it took her a moment to figure out why she was so warm. She recognised her own bedroom when she opened her eyes, but it took her longer to realise that she was not alone in it – and that Anthony's body was wrapped around hers. Well, some of his body; his cast-covered leg and arm were awkwardly straight.

She tried really hard not to move. If she woke him up, it would surely be awkward, for they would have to acknowledge the fact that they had spent the night in the same bed together, even if nothing more had happened. And that they had woken curled up together.

And it would mean that it would all come to an end. She hadn't planned to share a bed with him, but she had to admit it was very pleasant to be wrapped in his warm embrace.

But she couldn't stay still forever. Eventually, her right side became numb, and she had to stretch. When she turned, he was awake, and she couldn't quite read the expression in his eyes.

"Morning," she said, her voice a little croaky.

"Good morning." His voice was, of course, as smooth and rich as ever.

"I must've fallen asleep..." Hannah said with an embarrassed half-shrug. Did he remember telling her, asking her, to stay? And why *had* he asked her to stay? Did he want her there? Or was it just a suggestion, since it was late and she had given up her bed for him?

"I'm not sure I remember the end of the film," he said with a smile, stretching. The contact between them was broken, and Hannah instantly felt colder.

She wanted to tell him that she felt something; that what was between them was more than just friendship, at least on her side. That she would happily stay wrapped in his arms every night if she could.

But why were the words so hard to summon?

"Do you want a coffee?" she asked instead.

CHAPTER THIRTY

That evening, after a very pleasant day spent wandering through a local park with Anthony reluctantly using his wheelchair, they decided to order a takeaway and open a bottle of wine.

"I'm going to have to go back to work on Monday," she said as she poured them both a full glass of red. "Will you be okay here on your own? I know it's not easy for you to get out and about..."

He reached over and put a hand over hers. Dear God, did he know what he did to her? Or were these touches just innocent, something he did without thinking?

"Don't worry about it," he said, taking his hand back. "I'll be fine – I really appreciate you taking this week off to make sure I'm okay. Seriously. It's more than I could ever have expected."

Hannah sipped her wine before answering. "I don't mind. It's been nice having you here." But was it truly pathetic of her to be taking care of a man who had no idea how she felt about him?

A man she really shouldn't feel so much for?

"Well, it's appreciated. But if I'm honest, I hadn't even planned to take this long off. I can work remotely... So I won't go out anywhere while you're gone. I'll just get on with work. And you must tell me if I'm overstaying my welcome..."

Hannah quickly shook her head. She was finding it hard to imagine being alone in her flat again, if she was honest. "You can stay as long as you need to. I don't want you going home and falling, or trying to get around and doing more damage to your arm or leg. Or adding another concussion to the list."

"It has been a lot easier with help," he admitted. "Not that I'd ever tell my mother that. I can't wait until these casts are off, though. They make getting around so difficult. And when I'm in bed, I fall asleep and forget they're there, and end up with this ridiculously heavy limb refusing to cooperate."

She blushed at the simple thought that they had shared that bed last night. What had become of her? She had never, ever in her whole life acted this way because of a man. She had never over-analysed every conversation, questioned every kiss, read into every touch. He was some kind of drug that she just couldn't quit. And being around him felt so good... But she was rather worried that, in the end, the withdrawal would be extremely hard.

The food arrived, and they were quiet for a while as they tucked into the Chinese takeaway they'd ordered. They shared dishes, which was a pleasant change for Hannah, who normally just ordered the same thing every time, not wanting to risk getting something she didn't like or having loads left over that had to be binned.

Hannah was opening a second bottle before she realised it. It was more than she normally drank at home, but she didn't have work in the morning, so what did it matter?

"I can't believe Christi was that naughty as a child," Hannah said with a laugh. "She just doesn't seem the type!"

"Well, maybe not naughty, but she certainly got into a lot of scrapes. I guess being the youngest of four, and us all being brothers...it was more noticeable when she got stuck up a tree or rearranged the neighbours' gnomes into some inappropriate tableau than it was when it was one of us." There was a twinkle in his eye when he spoke of his childhood and his siblings, and Hannah wondered what it would have been like to grow up with brothers and sisters. She had always liked being an only child; she liked her own space, she liked peace and quiet when she wanted it, and she had been the sole focus of her parents' attention.

Of course, that meant now that she was still the sole focus – and the only one her mother had to try to marry off to someone suitable. It was like living in an Austen novel.

"It sounds fun, your childhood."

"Yeah, it was. Mum and Dad were always working, although I understand that more now that I'm a lawyer myself. But we had plenty of fun amongst the four of us."

Hannah sipped her wine. "Do you miss seeing them regularly, now that you're all so spread out? Especially with Mark in California."

Anthony considered the question for a moment. "I do... But I've got to admit, I'm so busy with work, I don't notice the time passing. Is that terrible?"

Hannah shook her head. "Not at all. I'm the same, but I don't think everyone gets it. For some people, like my parents, it's just a job... They can't understand loving it, being consumed by it."

Anthony nodded. "My parents understand, they just think I should be able to manage more than I am. But sometimes, I wonder if they've got a point..."

Hannah frowned. "Anthony, you're really successful. Don't start questioning it all just because your parents want you to settle down–"

"I know. I'm not saying they're totally right. But... I guess I'm thinking when I'm sixty, do I want to still be working every hour under the sun with no one to go home to at night?"

Hannah couldn't disagree with him, because she had the same thoughts herself. Would she always love her job as much as she did? She hoped so. But if a day came when she couldn't work, or didn't want to work... Then where would she be?

"I don't want to be alone forever, you know?" Anthony said with a shrug. "Maybe that's why I jumped in without thinking, with Sam..." He downed the rest of his wine and gave her a sad smile. "Sorry, the red wine makes me maudlin. Maybe I should switch to water."

Hannah didn't know if it was the rush of the alcohol just hitting her, or his sincere words, or the fact that she felt so similar, but she reached out and took his hand, desperate for some contact between them. "You won't be alone forever. I'm sure of it."

The kiss seemed inevitable at that point. She didn't know who started it. She didn't know how much it was fuelled by wine, or loneliness, or just sheer proximity – but they managed to shove their wineglasses onto the coffee table without spilling any drops of ruby-red liquid, their lips still locked, and Hannah found herself awkwardly perched in Anthony's lap, trying to keep her weight off his broken leg, him keeping his broken arm out of the way, as his good hand entwined in her hair, pulling her tighter.

The haze that had settled over her mind from the alcohol was burned away with that kiss. She wrapped both arms around his neck, pulled herself closer, revelled in the solid feeling of his chest, and in that moment, nothing else mattered. Not the fact that this was complicating things, not the fact that he might regret it, not the fact that she was scared to even admit her feelings to herself, let alone him. She wanted this, she wanted him, and she wasn't going to overthink it.

When they eventually pulled apart, both gasping for breath, their eyes locked. This had to mean something. She couldn't go back again to pretending that this wasn't what she wanted. She had to be brave.

Yes, it might end in heartbreak. But if she didn't try, she'd never know.

"How much of our relationship was fake, for you?" she asked when she could eventually speak, her chest still rising and falling faster than it should. "Because it wasn't all fake for me, Anthony."

He smiled and brushed his fingers through her hair. She leant into the touch, her heart hammering, needing an answer.

"I'm not sure," he said, and although it wasn't exactly the answer she wanted, at least he wasn't pushing her away. "But I know one thing... There was nothing fake about that kiss."

Her heart racing, she leant forward and pressed her lips to his once more, before saying the words that had been on her mind for a long while. "Somehow...this" – and she wasn't only referring to the phenomenal kiss – "is more real than anything I've had in a long time."

She presumed he agreed, because he pulled her to him and kissed her until she couldn't think straight.

The next morning, when she woke up in her own bed, Anthony beside her, she did not worry about staying still. She didn't think he was going anywhere. She leant against his chest, and they lazily kissed good morning, and Hannah was very glad she had nowhere to be. She had missed work, while she'd been off taking care of Anthony – but right now there was nowhere she'd rather be.

"So," Anthony said, when they sat in bed with coffees that Hannah had fetched from the kitchen, since there was no way Anthony could currently carry more than one cup at a time. Even with one, there was a decent chance he'd spill it on account of his broken leg. "We give this a go? For real?"

She looked up at him and smiled. "I don't want to pretend any more."

"Me neither."

"But I have to warn you..." she said, resolving that she was going to go into this with her boundaries clear. "I work crazy hours. I'm not going to give up my job, I'm not going to cut back on my hours, I'm not going to move..."

He laughed. "I work crazy hours. And I'm not going to give up my job. So let's see if we can make things work without changing who we are fundamentally – does that seem like a good plan?"

She snuggled in against his chest, feeling content. "A very good plan indeed."

EPILOGUE

There had been a time when Hannah would have hated the thought of going to a wedding. Having to get the time off work, having to find a date or turning up without one, finding a dress, having to see family, and dealing with their numerous views on her life. It was something she would have dreaded – or even simply avoided altogether.

And yet...for the year that she had attended such family functions as Anthony's pretend girlfriend, she had actually started to enjoy them. It was fun to get drunk with family members, to see people she hadn't seen in a long time, to let her hair down and get dressed up. It was fun spending time with Anthony, too...

And now? Now she was sitting in her boyfriend's sports car – the one he had bought to replace the one he'd written off previously – winding their way down to Devon for a summer wedding, in the very place where it had all begun.

"Mum wants us to go for dinner on our way back home," Hannah said. "Is that all right, or are you rushing back for work?"

"I've got to work first thing the next day, so as long

as we're not too late, it's fine by me."

"I've got a six a.m. shift the next day, so we won't be late. Besides, you know the amount of time I can spend with my parents is limited..."

Anthony chuckled. "Well, they love me, so that makes it a bit easier, doesn't it?"

Hannah rolled her eyes. "Don't get too smug. You know your parents love me. You're not the only one who can be the favourite."

"I know that. Besides, with Mark and Logan still single, most of the comments about where people's lives are heading aren't directed at me any more. So that's nice."

Hannah laughed. "Well, except for the grandchildren one – I think we'll be getting that forever."

They had discussed the possibility of children. In the year they'd been together, properly, they had both found that they liked to have things set out ahead of time, so everyone knew what to expect. Since neither of them wanted children right now, they had decided to put the idea on the back burner. Not that their parents fully accepted that, but they would just have to deal with it.

The tiny village of Hope Cove was as picturesque as Hannah remembered. Even though she still could not fathom why anyone would want to live there permanently, the beauty of it was not lost on her, and she couldn't help but harbour some romantic feelings towards the place that had brought her and Anthony together, leading to the year of happiness they'd been enjoying so far.

"We made good time," Anthony said as he parked in the steep car park of the hotel where Oscar and Christi had married. The wedding the following day was to be in the local church, with the celebration held at the hotel. Anthony had been quick to book them a room so they could enjoy the party without worrying about how they were going to get back.

It was, for once, a wedding where neither of their parents would be in attendance, so they had no one to look out for. Christi and Oscar had offered for them to stay at the B&B or even the campsite, but they were quite happy in a hotel room.

"Is Ava a flower girl?" Hannah asked. "Or is Rose? Or both? "I know Christi's the maid of honour..."

"I've got no idea," Anthony said with a shrug. "To be honest, I've been worrying more about my best man speech."

Hannah entwined her arm with his as they approached the desk to check-in. "You'll be great. You're a natural public speaker. All that time in front of a jury – you've had plenty of practice."

Anthony groaned. "I can do public speaking. It's the thought of making people laugh that's more of an issue. I'm not sure I'm very funny."

"Hannah! Anthony! You're here," a voice called, and Hannah turned to see Ivy, the beautiful bride-to-be, with her long brown hair plaited down her back and a broad smile on her face.

"We didn't expect to see you here," Hannah said, returning Ivy's embrace. "Are you all ready for tomorrow?"

Ivy looked radiant. She had wanted to be married for a long time, and Hannah wasn't sure she'd ever seen someone so happy. There wasn't a hint of pre-wedding jitters or cold feet in sight.

"I think so. I'm just here checking on a couple of

last-minute details – Alfie's over at his parents' holiday home. You know, so we don't see each other the night before the wedding."

Hannah nodded. It seemed a rather antiquated tradition to her, especially since they lived together and shared a child, but she wasn't going to say anything to burst her bubble of happiness.

"Is Alfie doing okay?" Anthony asked, joining them.

"Nervous about his speech, I think."

Hannah laughed. "Anthony's the same. I told him he's a lawyer, he's used to it – and Alfie doesn't even have to make people laugh, does he? Just sound sincere..."

She shrugged. "I'm glad I don't have to make a speech. I'm nervous enough about walking down the aisle in front of people, in case I trip."

Hannah was very happy for the sweet, shy girl. From what she'd heard from Christi, Ivy's previous boyfriend had treated her like she was totally forgettable, and now she was marrying a man who looked at her like he'd won the grand prize.

"Do you need help with anything?" Hannah asked. "We're just going to put our stuff in our room, then sit around until dinner, I guess..."

Ivy shook her head. "No, thanks. I think everything is under control, and Dad's outside waiting to take me home. He's got Rose too, so I mustn't be too long. She'll have talked his ear off – always got questions, that one."

Once they had deposited their belongings and hung up their suit and dress so they wouldn't get too wrinkled before the following day, Hannah and Anthony walked downstairs hand in hand, reminiscing over the last wedding they had attended together.

"As long as no drunk woman randomly kisses me

tomorrow," Anthony said with a laugh, "I think I'll be okay."

Hannah rolled her eyes and batted his arm. "I thought you were a random man. If I'd realised you were the bride's brother, maybe I would have thought better of it. Found someone less complicated."

He pulled her towards him and pressed a kiss to her lips at the bottom of the stairs. "I'm glad you didn't pick someone less complicated," he said.

She smiled up at him. "Me too."

When they reached the lobby, Anthony glanced up at the clock. "It's still early. And the weather is beautiful. Fancy a wander on the beach before dinner?"

"Go on then – but I'm not swimming."

The hotel was nestled in the cliffs, and they walked down the steep hill to the little beach where the waves were crashing against the break wall. There were some people swimming, and children playing on the beach. It was only small, but they took off their shoes and socks and wandered across the sand barefoot, enjoying the summer sunshine and the fresh sea air.

"You don't get that in London," Anthony commented.

"No, you don't," Hannah agreed. "But there's a lot that you can get in London that you don't get down here."

Anthony nodded.

"Do you mind that we're looking for houses in London, and not elsewhere?" Hannah asked, suddenly worried he was going to declare he wanted to up sticks and move to the countryside.

"I told you," he said, squeezing her hand, "I'm happy to leave Oxford. I want to live with you, and London makes sense."

She smiled and snuggled up against him. When they'd first got together, she'd said she wouldn't move – but when it came down to it, she wanted to live with him too. It worked out perfectly that he was happy to relocate, so she could still be close to the hospital, but this time, they would have a house together.

She wanted to hold firm to her boundaries, to not lose herself – and yet she rather thought that if he'd said he wanted to move to Devon, she was far too much in over her head to have refused to go.

Thankfully, that didn't seem to be his inclination.

They sat on the sand for a while, watching the waves and the children playing.

"It is a beautiful place for a wedding," Anthony said. "And I'm not surprised Ivy and Alfie chose here too, with how much Ivy loves the beach."

"Did you ever think Alfie would end up moving to Devon permanently, when you first came down here together and stayed at Christi's?" Hannah asked.

Anthony laughed. "No way – but I guess love does strange things... And he seems really happy."

Hannah nodded and then leant her head against Anthony's shoulder. "He really does. They both do. I'm happy for them."

"Do you think you'd ever want to get married in a church?" Anthony asked, and Hannah was rather taken aback by the sudden question.

"I don't think so..." she said slowly. "I'm not religious, so..." She shrugged. Where had that come from?

"Me neither. I think I'd quite like to elope... Get married in some city abroad. What do you think? Would you be up for that?"

Hannah's heart felt as though it was in her throat. This was uncharted territory.

"Anthony... Are you... Are you asking me to marry you?"

She twisted her neck and looked up at him, trying to read his expression.

He cocked his head to one side. "I guess I am."

Hannah laughed, partly from shock.

"What do you think?" Anthony asked in his smooth, deep voice, sounding totally unruffled by the question.

Hannah sat up fully. "I think that I would be up for an elopement. And that if I were to get married, I would want to keep my own surname."

Anthony nodded.

"And I also think," Hannah said, unable to keep the smile from her face, "that if you want me to marry you, you'd better ask me properly. There's nothing fake about this relationship anymore – and I think I deserve better than a half-baked proposal."

He grinned at her admonishment and turned to her, leaning on one knee. "You are entirely right. As always. Hannah Martin – will you marry me?"

And she didn't have to think for even one second before throwing her arms around him, pressing her lips to his, and saying, "Yes!"

Want to catch up with Christi, Oscar, Ivy, Alfie, Anthony, & Hannah, plus see another King sibling fall in love? Pre-order 'Coming Home to Kingsbridge' today! mybook.to/Kingsbridge

AFTERWORD

Thank you so much for reading 'Happily Ever After in Hope Cove'! Hope Cove is such a beautiful part of the South Hams. There is a real hotel that looks out over the sea, although I've invented some of the features of my Hope Cove hotel! Although Hannah and Anthony don't want to settle down there, it will always be the place where they found each other. I loved heading back to Devon – both for research and in the book! – to bring you this story, and I hope you enjoyed catching up with all the characters, as well as meeting some new faces.

If you want to know what happens next, sign up for the pre-order for book 4, 'Coming Home to Kingsbridge', today! Mybook.to/Kingsbridge. You can also join my mailing list for news of releases, sales, and what's going on in my life! Tiny.cc/paulinyi

Thanks again for reading, your support means everything.

Rebecca

BOOKS IN THIS SERIES

Dreaming of Devon

Sunsets Over Salcombe

Broken-Hearted On Blackpool Sands

Happily Ever After In Hope Cove

Comng Home To Kingsbridge

BOOKS BY THIS AUTHOR

The Worst Christmas Ever?

Lawyers And Lattes

Feeling The Fireworks

The Best Christmas Ever

Trouble In Tartan

Summer Of Sunshine

Healing The Heartbreak

Dancing Till Dawn

At The Stroke Of Thirty

Life Begins At Thirty

Printed in Dunstable, United Kingdom

76554312R00139